DEAD ARTIST

DEAD ARTIST

A Novel

by

Ivan Jenson

HEN HOUSE PRESS, NEW YORK

HEN HOUSE PRESS
Published by Hen House Press

Copyright 2011 by Ivan Jenson

ISBN: 978-0-9834604-8-0

10 9 8 7 6 5 4 3 2 1

To my father who sat shirtless in the summertime, typing out on his Smith Corona all four hundred handwritten pages of my first novel, written at the age of 13.

To my mother who each morning at 5:00AM reads my pages with red pen in hand.

And lastly to Dr. B who always said, "Good" when I told him I had been writing but never lived long enough to see my dreams come true.

DEAD ARTIST

Chapter One

In the heat of the afternoon Milo stood, unschooled, untutored, untamed hair, self taught. He was an artist.

The summer dropped light on this small town like a hot white sheet straight out of the dryer. The movers were at work wrapping all of Milo's paintings in bubble wrap. They were taking the paintings Milo had created and shipping them to his new dealer's home in New York City.

One of the movers was lanky, shy, and looked eighteen. The other one was bald and had his gaze fixed on one of Milo's large-scale paintings when he said, "This one here, this woman you painted with the cascading hair, she looks just like my wife right down to the pouting lips, if you had just made her eyes green, I tell you I would have bought this painting on the spot. Who is this?"

"She came straight from my imagination. I didn't use a model at all." Milo lied.

"You got some imagination there," the bald mover said. He was tall and thin, and all smiles. The day had clouded up and it hailed in June. The hail was the size of silver dollars.

"Look at that weather," the mover said. "It must be a sign that something special is about to happen for you."

Milo hardly listened to the man. His mind was preoccupied. Watching the hail fall outside the garage studio, he began to feel almost hypnotized.

Now, in his mid forties, Milo felt like a woman with her biological clock ticking and desperately longing for marriage and children. He thought back to the women he had loved in New York. He pictured them now, freshly showered, hair sleek and dark like a fresh pot of coffee. Suddenly it was all rushing back to Milo. The days of abundant sex and money. It had been a long time since he was last famous and now his second chance was coming. It was like a second wind. He could hear in his mind the voice of Nick, his new art dealer and how just a couple of weeks ago he had said, "I am going to make Milo Sonas a household name." Nick had said this to Milo at the Kennedy Airport terminal, and then added, "I am going to make you lots and lots of money. All you have to do is paint, have fun and enjoy the ride."

What a trip that had been! Nick had wined and dined Milo and taken him to the best VIP strip clubs, given him a hundred dollars and told him to get lap dances. And Milo stayed at Nick's house which was like a museum dedicated to Milo's paintings, collected by Nick over the years

Milo hadn't painted in half a decade. And when he saw those early works, he said to himself, "So that's what I am, I am an artist after all."

The movers were lifting Milo's *Portrait of Van Gogh* and placing it in a cardboard box. Here in this garage in his mother's home, he had painted these works. Being a lonely widow, his mother enjoyed having him around. While his father was alive, Milo never in his heart acknowledged him as his sole father. Instead Milo insisted that he had many fathers. One of them was Picasso... the robust, stalky, prolific cigarette puffing genius who married classic beauties twenty years younger than himself. Milo had a hard time modeling himself after his father who was a failed novelist and who, during the last half of his life, toiled on the rewrite of the same novel, and was still submitting it to agents when he died, fortunately enabling him to avoid the disappointment of the inevitable rejection letters.

Milo had always postponed and sacrificed all worldly possessions and status in society in anticipation of the time when true success would find him. He knew right away that school was not for him, that it was not necessary. In school he played the role of the manic class clown.

His sixth grade class once took a week-long field trip to a Southern California mountain camp. On their first morning in the campsite, Milo dressed in nothing but a sheet from his bunk bed, stood at the edge of a cliff and pretended to be Jesus, gesturing as if he had the power to make the sun rise. He commanded it to rise, chanting, "I am your Messiah! I am your Messiah!" Even the camp counselors broke a smile. However Milo was not punished by his teacher, she thought it was an imaginative, and historically accurate prank.

Milo had the opposite of paranoia. He now believed the entire world was conspiring to help him. And so he coined the word, "Posanoia."

There was a time when he felt that success eluded him. This bothered him so much that, one December six years ago, he let his mind get trapped like a hamster in a treadmill of obsession and no matter how close he got to having it all it was always "close but no banana." Once in the The Pinebrook Mental ward reception area, he saw a bowl of fruit on a desk next to the receptionist. He demanded to have a banana. The staff told him the fruit was just for show and not for the patients' consumption. Milo pleaded. He said there was a reason why he wanted the banana, an important reason. So they gave the banana to him. That was the only time he got the banana in life, or so it seemed.

But now Nick had promised him the whole bunch.

As Milo continued to watch the movers wrap his canvases, Milo considered calling a friend and saying, "take a look at me now." But Milo lost all his friends. Even the one he vowed to be friends with all his life. They had met in an elementary school coat room and promised to be friends for life. Milo through the years entertained his best friend with his humor but things stopped being funny when that friend started earning a six figure salary and Milo was still selling his art on the streets of New York.

Milo had always been funny at parties. "The life of the party" that's what they called him. Blatantly insulting guests with sharp wicked improv, some friends paid for him to entertain at their weddings just so he could spice and lighten up the event. But in the end the joke was on Milo. He ended up living in poverty in a dive in New York City. His only relief came when young girls would visit his "cave." His studio was called a cave because it was dark and cavernous and had only one small window. It was a storefront on the ground floor, with a front door that opened to the sidewalk. Milo remembered one girl with theatrically made up eyes who had asked him, "Don't you want a wife and a family?"

"I can't afford any of that," he had said.

And then she put the whip cream on his naked body.

There was a time when women tracked him down, and followed him to hotel suites. They hunted him. When he was famous.

Milo's thoughts were interrupted.

Milo heard his mother calling from her upstairs bedroom. He went back in the house, headed up the stairs and entered the attic room where she was sitting up in bed. "How are they doing down there? Are they doing a good job?"

"Yes they are, everything is fine."

"Come here," his mother said.

He sat down on the bed and she took his hand.

"You will find someone and have everything. Don't worry Milo. Looks like I won't last long enough to watch it. I have noticed how all your life you are thinking about things, no matter what is happening around you, your mind is always somewhere else. Try to, as they say, to be in the here and now."

Milo's mother was devastated by her illness. Her feet were swollen from lack of circulation. She had quit smoking a year ago, but it was too late.

Milo was thinking about how much he would have liked his mother to meet his new wife. The problem was, he hadn't met her yet himself.

"I better get downstairs, and oversee what the art movers are doing," he said. Sometimes it was just too much to be near her.

IVAN JENSON

Chapter Two

Milo sat on his second-hand sofa in the garage and continued to watch the movers wrap up his paintings, and thought back to the ragtag days when he was a street artist. He missed the hustle. He missed systematically handing out cards to every pretty girl he saw. He used lines on the girls like, "You look Picasso-esque. You look like a woman from a Fellini film. You look like a painting I made last night." One night in Washington Square Park, a girl warned him that she had mace in her pocket. So he backed off. Sitting on his second-hand sofa, Milo thought, he would never have girl trouble again.

Fame is something paid for and arranged. And the arrangements were now being made for Milo Sonas.

Just months before, Nick paid for Milo to fly out to the east coast. He showed Milo a good time. Besides the strip clubs, he took Milo out to a Brazilian Churrascaria in Times Square where waiters with sword sized knives sliced slabs of beef, lamb, pork and chicken. Milo and Nick indulged like carnivorous Romans.

Nick had said, "I am doing this all for you, because I think you deserve it."

It took twenty years of selling on sidewalks to get here.

As his new paintings were being packed he thought back to how it all began.

Milo was the last child living at home. Each one of his six brothers and sisters had found someone or something and flown the coop. He had been especially close with his sister Luna. But at the age of nineteen

7

Luna found someone too. She met him when she stubbed her toe during a vacation in Costa Rica -- he was the ER doctor that treated her. She never came home again. Their mother was very close to Luna and when Luna left home she started acting erratic. A crisis team came at 5:00 am. The counselor said, "A family is like an organism that sometimes splits apart and one member feels the strain the most." The doctor gave Mrs. Sonas pills to relax her so that she could sleep.

One night his mother took all the pills at once. She claimed she only wanted to sleep, but it was perceived as a suicide attempt. She was taken to the County Hospital Psychiatric Ward. "Get me out of here," she pleaded a few hours into her mental ward lockdown. "Whatever you do, get me out of here now!" So her family got her out.

When she came back home the crisis team came to visit again and the counselor told her, "It's okay, you are feeling the pain of a loss."

"Yes," she said, "it is like a hole in my chest. What can I do to fill it up again?"

"You can't fill it up again. There will always be a void. You have to learn to live with it."

Milo's mother's eyes looked so hollow that night, like Grandmother's eyes looked before she died. It looked like the angels forgot to come.

The Sonas family were a lot like gypsies. After Luna left home, Milo, his mother and his father moved into that house in Pelham, in October. His father was retired from a job he never had and was working sporadically on his novel again. To support the family, Mrs. Sonas cooked for a nunnery.

Then came that fateful day when Milo threw color on paper, grabbed some rope from the garage, and took the Metro North to New York City. He strung his paintings on a line. Everything changed.

That cosmic aura of success touched him. He was an instant hit on the New York streets.

Luna drove up to the garage. Smiling, she got out of her car. She could never have anticipated this comeback for him. When Milo had first come to Gold Haven he was a total mess. She had waited for him at the airport. He looked heavier, unshaven, and sported a weary smile.

Luna:

Look at my brother now. It was just five years ago that he arrived at the Gold Haven Airport terminal looking like a castaway wearing clothing that didn't fit. In fact my brother Milo looked like he was wearing a dead man's clothing. My husband drove us all home and he said, "Milo I understand what you are going through, you have arrived at middle life and now you see that your dreams are not going to come true and that you will never achieve the heights in your career again. So your dreams are dead and yet you still have half a life to live. What do you do now? Look if I had lived the life that you had led, I couldn't have hung on as long as you did. I would have committed suicide long ago."

Those were my husband's exact words. But Martin was only trying to be honest. He may have thought he was being helpful. But I think he was being unwittingly harsh. And you should have seen the look on Milo's face when he heard Martin's speech. It looked like the angels hadn't come...

But what can anyone do when somebody is having a nervous breakdown?

But soon the new paintings would arrive at the collector's house. And Milo would soon make it out of Gold Haven, Michigan.

This was sure to be his last summer in this small town which felt so dead. All its residents had headed to summer cottages by Michigan lakes. The gym where he worked out and prepared for fame had been deserted. By day reading books like *The Secret*, *Think and Grow Rich* and a book on ESP, by night, in his room he raised his arms in the air, as the ESP book directed. And with arms raised high, Milo called forth the cosmic forces of the universe to transform his life. He longed to see the end of his heretofore unending loneliness and excruciating alienation.

It was because of his mother that Milo got discovered in New York in the first place.

At first as street-artist-in-the-eighties he had wished to be as famous as Andy Warhol or Keith Haring. And he was complaining to a girl, "All the big artists are showing in the clubs. Every artist wants to have a painting in a club called Pantheon."

Just then his mother called and said, "How would you like to have a painting at the Pantheon?" The Pantheon was the most famous club in the world. It was perfect synchronicity. His mother worked for a catering company, and a painting was needed behind a Sushi bar at a fashion event.

So mother Sonas sewed together two canvases and Milo created a ten foot by ten foot painting, called *Man of the Eighties*. He remembered entering the club and seeing his painting as the song Su-Su-Sudio played. It was his mother who told him to try to paint with foam brushes from the hardware store. That painting, at the top of the club, looked out at the sea of dancing people. Milo had arrived.

Now after a twenty year dry spell, it was all coming back. It had taken years of going to psychics, reading Louise Hay, working, wishing, praying, doing cosmic work. If he could just make it through this one last hurdle and reach the banana.

You see, the rest of his family would be arriving soon to Gold Haven, to pay their last respects to their mother.

Milo walked through the Woodbridge Mall where he spent many afternoons wandering. Perhaps he really was one of those people who simply wandered in the afternoon. Victoria's Secret mannequins beckoned him enticingly. And he couldn't take his eyes off the big blown up glossy photos of women in lingerie. Over by the food court a young mother with long legs and firmly defined calves ending in high heels was pushing a baby carriage. She was truly a trophy wife, pristine and skin yellow as a banana peel.

Milo watched her bend over to tend to her little girl. He is mesmerized.

"That's exactly the sort of wife that you must find," a voice with a heavy Spanish accent said to him. Milo turned around and there he was, Pablo Picasso sipping a Diet Coke through a straw. His skin was deeply tanned and orange colored and he wore loose linen shorts. He didn't look a day over eighty five. But as usual he made eighty five look like sixty five.

Milo was not at all surprised to see Pablo. These impromptu visitations had been happening for some time. Milo saw dead artists. These magical modern art mirages were a welcome relief from the mundane Muzak-drenched loitering that he indulged in most afternoons.

"So how are things going, Milo?"

"Nick will be flying me to New York for a photo shoot. I just need your opinion, do you think I should whiten my teeth. I will be meeting so many people."

Milo grinned for Pablo as one might in front of a dentist.

Pablo leaned in close and examined Milo's teeth. "For one thing you have a chive between your two front teeth."

"Oh shoot. Where? Here?" Milo said, turning his head to the side to give Pablo a clearer view.

"No the next tooth over."

"Here?"

"Yes."

"Is it gone?"

"No."

"Hold on."

Milo headed for the Woodbrige Mall restroom. He saw his tooth with the chive in the wall-spanning mirror. The chive was lettuce and it was bright green. "Damn it," he said to himself.

When Milo exited the restroom and rejoined Picasso, he said, "Well you never answered my question, are my teeth too yellow?"

"You're asking a man who has chained smoked all his life about yellow teeth, get over it. Hey look, there's a tanning center. Now that's something we both need, especially you, before your photo shoot. Can we go? Can we?" Picasso sounded childlike.

Picasso could be playful, but when he made a specific request, Milo always complied. Denying Picasso would yield either a temperamental fit, or a full-blown tantrum.

Pablo said, "In the Midwest I find it hard to maintain my French Riviera tan."

To appease Picasso they went to the tanning salon called Midnight Tan. They each headed toward their tanning booth. Milo stripped down to his underwear and stood in front of the lamps. Vents on either side of him blasted cool air on his body. He put on his glasses and chose the hip-hop channel for his headset. Before putting in the ear buds, he listened through the thin wall as Pablo chatted up the girl from the salon staff, the one with the tight black shorts and nose ring. When Pablo started groaning in ecstasy, Milo turned up the music.

When they came out, they both felt invigorated. Milo saw he had a message from Nick on his cell phone.

The shipment of new paintings has arrived. I received forty two paintings and one hundred drawings. This is a lot of inventory, and they should really do the trick for you. Hang in there, and very, very soon we'll get you out of the Midwest.

"It's my dealer Nick," Milo said to Pablo. "He loves the new paintings."

"I am happy for you," Pablo said. But Pablo was also envious. His life was over, it was Milo's turn now and he resented it. Yet he was willing to support Milo, that is why he had materialized. To help.

IVAN JENSON

Chapter Three

Luna:

...and so things are happening for Milo and I am happy for him. He gets this last minute second chance, a second wind. I have always thought that he had a charmed life anyhow. It is as if a lucky star has always shined over him. He got to live in his own world, I guess we all underestimated him. And all this is happening because one single person believes in him. Sometimes that is all it takes.

People once believed in me, I wasn't always a sloppy mother with a messy house. I didn't always have short hair, which I have to dye black now or it would be totally gray. I used to have flowing locks and a face straight out of a Da Vinci painting. Older people just loved me. I was the perfect child. I was on TV with Johnny Carson. He called me, "Love." They used to call me the "Love child."

Because I was in an ad for "Love" soap, it was gentle enough for babies but adults loved it too.

I remember Johnny Carson said, "You are a lovely girl. So tell me what do you like to do when you aren't starring in cute-as-a-button TV commercials about soap?"

I sat in that chair next to Johnny Carson with my feet propped up on a little cushioned stool they had brought out just for me. I was totally relaxed, when I said, "I love to be with my brother Milo, he is an artist."

"So would you say your brother is your hobby?"

"Yeah, he's my hubby."

The audience laughed, they didn't realize that I really was trying to say hobby, but it came out all wrong. Oh well, I didn't care.

Milo and I, we used to spend so much time together.

Milo, you used to draw and paint me even when I wasn't there. I was always amazed at your capacity to be alone, and to like it.

You taught yourself to be a painter. I used to envy you, you seemed to have so many fathers, Picasso, Leonardo, Michelangelo, Van Gogh, Lautrec. And then you tried to be so many things before you settled on the lonely life of being a visual artist. You used to write songs, okay, so your voice was not so pretty. Bob Dylan's voice isn't pretty either, and how about Rod Stewart's? He sounds like he has a sore throat all the time and everybody still loves him. I was your biggest fan...until I met my husband from San Jose at the age of nineteen. My real hubby. I was too young to decide to leave home. I left the family so early, and for an older man no less. Papa wouldn't talk to me for a year and he wouldn't talk to my husband.

Remember the crisis team told us that when families break apart one member always feels the pull.

Mom really suffered when I left home. But I just had to stay away, even when she tried to kill herself I wouldn't come to see her. Mom and I were just way too close.

You and I were too close too.

Remember how we looked alike Milo?

That afternoon on your ninth birthday when it was raining and you thought everyone forgot your birthday. And you came home soaked from the July rain and there we all were. We remembered after all! Momma, Papa, our brothers and sisters Amelia and Paul and Becky and Ray. And they gave you tubes of paint instead of toys. But then Ray ruined that day when he told you that some crazed maniac had taken a sledge hammer to Michelangelo's Pieta in the Vatican. I remember you were so upset, you wept for days. You have always had an old soul, Milo. And you also had what I thought could only be called a Michelangelo complex. I know there is no such thing, sure many boys had Oedipal complexes, you had a dose of that too. But it is not normal for a boy to watch Charlton Heston as Michelangelo in the Agony and the Ecstasy over and over again in your room. You were a prodigy at being obsessive.

My husband still looks like you Milo, that's what I first noticed about him. That similarity. It's a vibe, Milo, we all look the same, we all have big innocent eyes, thick lips, we look like Botticelli people. We look like we belong in another century. Another time. Another place. But at least my husband and I found a place that is proper and acceptable in this world. I have children, five of them. While you Milo crashed at friends' houses. Now it kills me that you live in that creepy hotel in Gold Haven. There was a time when you made everybody laugh. But then everybody kinda gave up on you without realizing it. We forgot about you. You fell between the cracks. But now that man named Nick who lives on the East Coast believes in you and your paintings and that is making all the difference. So it turns out you are going to be a household name. Well, I am happy for you. Kinda yes, and kinda no. It's hard on me because I have harbored the hope that one day I would be in a commercial again, or perhaps do some acting, even if it was just in a soap. I don't mean like Love Soap, I mean like as in a soap opera. But I don't have an agent, haven't had one in thirty years. It hurts a little that it is happening for you and not me. But I can take it. I have learned that as we get older, life humbles us.

I just wonder how Ray is going to react to your resurgence in the art world.

Chapter Four

Milo was imagining his agent unwrapping the paintings in New York. It all felt so strange, but he had to keep reminding himself that this is something that he had always wanted. This would be his last summer in Gold Haven, his last summer as a washed up artist, a modern day ne'er-do-well. Nobody would believe him if he were to tell them that a cosmic force has taken over his life. He could feel this full force in his chest, making his heart palpitate and his breathing short and shallow. But for now he still played the sport of extreme loneliness.

"I really hope you make a lot of money." The voice on the phone was brittle, soft, and it sounded old and gravelly. It was Dr. Hyatt.

Milo answered, "I just want to thank you for being here for me all these years."

"You're welcome."

Not many people have someone like Dr. Hyatt in their lives. But Milo did.

"I would like to see you when I come out to New York," Milo said.

"I'm afraid that won't be possible."

Dr. Hyatt was Milo's mentor, his wise old sage, his therapist, and sometimes, his verbal punching bag. Milo called him "Doctor" Hyatt even though the old man had lost his license years ago. Dr. Hyatt lost his psychiatric license when he prescribed Ativan indiscriminately to a patient and the patient became addicted. He also once had an affair with one of his young female charges. And now things were becoming even more dire for Dr. Hyatt. He said to Milo, "They passed a law in New York that requires all therapists to have a license to provide therapy. I think it is total bullshit, but that's the way it is. So we can no longer have office visits nor can you send me payments."

"Well I am living in Gold Haven, Michigan and you in New York, so it is unlikely we will have an office visit any time soon. But I can't believe I cannot pay you for your services. You mean I can never write that big thank you check for all the years you have been there for me?"

"That's right, you're off the hook."

"You know Dr. Hyatt, I never thought that it would really happen for me."

"Most success comes to a man in his middle years."

"And how have you been Dr. Hyatt?"

"I don't go out at night like I used to. And my back hurts. Old age sucks. But let's not talk about me, let's talk about you, Milo Sonas."

"I went to the local Mall with Picasso today, we went to a tanning salon."

"That's nice," the former doctor said.

"You still don't think I am crazy because I am friends with Picasso?"

"You don't sound crazy."

"But Picasso visits me, and we spend time together, we are friends and he is dead."

"Apparently for you he isn't. Listen I have another call I have to attend to. I'll be here at ten thirty if you need to talk some more."

"Dr. Hyatt, thank you, really, I mean it."

"You talk like I am going to die."

"Well you might, it could happen at any second."

"But it might not."

DEAD ARTIST

Milo may have had a Michelangelo complex as a boy, but then when he hit adolescence he developed a Picasso complex, a Van Gogh, and a Lolita complex all put together.

Now, it was a warm summer night and the fourth of July was drawing near. Yes, it would soon be Independence Day, and Van Gogh was in Gold Haven, Michigan watching VH1 and holding Milo's dog Moon. Vincent said, "You know, they have done psychological studies and found that those that don't have physical affection in their life, if these people are given paints, the paintings they make are more likely to be filled with a lot of pigment and texture. Lonely people paint with a brush loaded with paint. Maybe that's why both you and I paint with a loaded brush. But maybe now that your ship is coming in Milo, and when you find love, your paintings will become more smooth and graphic, because soon you will be bedding all those beautiful truffles. All that I ask is that you don't forget about me when I am gone."

"Where are you going?" Milo asks casually.

"Oh, I don't know. I am not sure why I said that."

Picasso stepped out of the bathroom. "Of course Milo should forget you. What good will it do the world to have another artist as victim? My advice to you Milo is to completely disassociate yourself from Vincent. But I do advise you to keep making those Pop style versions of Van Gogh, because those suckers are going to make you a millionaire."

"You guys, I need to get some sleep," Milo said, snatching Moon from Van Gogh and transferring her to his bed.

Before hitting the sack there was one ritual he just had to do. Milo lit a candle, and then he stood in the center of his room raised his hands into the air, and verbally called forth the cosmic forces of the universe.

He felt a power shoot through him. Yes this was finally working.

Yes!

Chapter Five

Late June

Ray:

It isn't often that a person feels like they could just kill somebody. But I do. What that means is that I am willing to sacrifice my freedom to end someone else's.

Summer makes people do things. Maybe it is the summer that is making me want to do this. People say I am an angry person. Damn right I am angry. Nobody ever gave me anything. Nada. I have always had to work, and work hard, I've even driven a cab in New York and I had no qualms with doing that. Since then I have become a painter. Not an artist mind you, but a house painter. There is a difference. Artists use a full spectrum of color and design and express themselves on canvas after canvas...but house painters, those like me, simply paint white on walls. And it really hurts when you are a painter and you have a brother who is an artist. It's enough to drive one mad crazy. Meanwhile right now I am getting wind that my own little brother is suddenly slated to be some kind of shooting star in the art world. Give me a break! For the past five years he has been completely and totally down and out, living in a one-star hotel, and I remember how he calls me and says he has a dream of one day moving to Chicago or back to New York and I told him, "maybe there is a halfway house you can move to." Look I know it was a callous thing to say. But shit, that guy has always had some kind of lucky star shining down on his life, even when he is all fucked up it seems to be up there and glowing. The guy used to just go out on the streets of New York and he would get totally showered in cash, don't know how he did it. I was jealous of all that money coming at him while I drove a damn cab. I know the guy has had it tough, having that nervous breakdown or whatever it was he had. Knocked him right off his feet. It looked like he was down for good and I will be honest, I felt kinda good about it. It gave me a chance to maybe get ahead in life. But I just keep on painting houses. I work alone. I tape the interior walls, plaster up the gaps and lay down the tarp, and if there is a Mrs. who is home while I work, a Mrs. who is delirious of the fact that her MasterCard can buy her the manual labor of a guy like me; who is by the way, if I say so myself, ruggedly handsome. I am like a male hustler that costs forty an hour, and I paint shirtless to boot. I wear a mask because of the latex fumes, but sometimes I think that the fumes get to the wives, because that's why I have slept with more than just a few of 'em. And why not have a little afternoon delight?

Milo has always said that he had many fathers, Picasso, Van Gogh, Michelangelo to name a few, I don't know why he couldn't just focus on the one true father we did have. I know why, because our father was a welfare dad. A kept man. A stay at home Papa, long before that ever became fashionable. Okay, so he fancied himself to be a freelance writer. He was always writing and re-writing, editing and re-editing a novel he titled "Cuckold to Contessa." I read some pages, it was something about his nymphomaniac first wife who fucked, or so it seemed, every man in my father's life at the time. Apparently this dame fucked my father's best friend, his brother, his electrician, etc. Our father died unpublished. I guess that everybody in this family has made a desperate stab at success, I call it small time desperation.

Milo's stab at the big time came when he went out on a street corner in the early eighties and became an overnight success, it only took him six months to turn into an East Village phenomena. The guy rubs shoulders with everybody from Keith Haring, Andy Warhol and even Basquiat stops by and says hello to him while he sold his paintings out there on West Broadway. He becomes best friends with a billionaire, and almost makes it all the way. But then the stock market crashes, the art world dries up, and my brother's refrain becomes, "Close, but no banana."

Jeez!

IVAN JENSON

Chapter Six

These most certainly were the last days that Milo would hear the operatic basso of his mother's voice echoing through the house as she made phone calls to various family members and relayed current events. His mother relayed gossip about cousin Mandy who was no longer little, no, she was all grown up now and tall as a shooting bamboo and getting straight A's in high school while also winning tennis tournaments and it really wasn't fair that she should be tall, pretty and smart. And my how her grandson Donny could shovel down food, his cheeks bulging with every heaping mouthful. The boy was only sixteen and already he weighed over two hundred pounds, and oh, the way he talked about girls! Like they were nothing but playthings, Luna even overheard him refer to them as bitches and ho's. And Hilda is already nineteen and going to study abroad in Paris, no less, and her poor good son Paul, you know he is pushing sixty, how she feels for him. He's a handyman now, at least he is no longer a courier, but anyhow he makes good money playing his violin at weddings on weekends. He is happy, yes happy. He just took a discount cruise to Europe with his wife, okay so it was a cruise with senior citizens but old people can be sweet, and at least poor Paul got to scuba dive in Monaco. And Becky keeps trying to make her first movie, and Luna, sometimes she worries about her. She doesn't think one ever gets over being a child star, maybe it was all a big mistake. Everyone is just so busy...and she talks about her youngest, yes Milo, things are changing for him the most. Pretty soon if things keep going the way they are going, he won't even talk to us anymore, but maybe it will just be a false alarm, there have been so many close calls for him, when we thought he was really going to get there...he has gotten so close, and I do wish so much that this time it really happens.

Mrs. Sonas was jaded from twenty years of looking out for Milo. It had been a long time since he was last famous. But this time it looked like it was really going to happen again, and so she took a sudden interest in her own health and well being and she began to take walks on the treadmill in her bedroom. She was booking appointments with her doctor, taking her vitamins, hoping to stay alive long enough to witness Milo's success. But it was during one of these physical check ups up that she was told she was dying.

Nick called Milo and said, "I don't want to get your hopes up too high, but I think I am going to rent a gallery in the Chelsea District to display your art during the international auction. Does that sound good to you?"

"Sure," Milo said. "That sounds fantastic."

Meanwhile Milo was thinking, will mother be alive to see it all? Mothers, they just don't last...it is like that with mothers.

Milo remembered having dinner with his New York lawyer and his wife and her mother. This woman was vivacious and looked healthy and filled with life. His lawyer, who he had met on the street, lived in a villa in Mamaroneck. At one point Milo cracked an innocent joke, he didn't remember the punch line, or the set up. But later he wondered if this joke was perhaps at somebody else's expense, maybe it was, because the lady died the next day. In the back of his mind he always felt he was responsible for her death in some eerie way.

Milo had ordered a twelve inch sub at Blimpie's and his plan was to share it with his mother. When he arrived at her house Moon was licking his mother's lips. For her mouth was open, her eyes were closed, and she wasn't breathing. And just like that it seemed the era of his mother was over, and he dialed 911 as she lay breathless on the living room floor. After he got off the phone with Emergency his mother suddenly spoke in a voice as weak as a clogged vent, "I had a cousin, I'm not sure if he is still alive, his mother was quite beautiful. They lived in Mexico City and he was very close with his mother, and you know something, that is okay. He also, like you Milo, could not find a wife for most of his life. His mother lived just long enough, or so it seemed, for him to find somebody. The girl he met was a simple girl, a street vendor, she sold flowers on the plaza. In any case she looked just like his mother. He brought her home to meet his mother. They ate rice and beans and tapas. That evening they played cards and drank tequila. That night his girlfriend slept over. They made love and conceived their first child. In the morning they woke to the smell of four sunny side up eggs burning on the stove. His mother lay dead on the kitchen floor, wearing an apron."

"Is that what you are going to do when I fall in love?" Milo asked, looking down at his mother resting peacefully on the carpet.

"It's just family lore, that's all. But it is true, I think the universe will sigh with relief when you find love. By the way, are you sure you want to have a gallery show in New York City? Isn't that what chewed you up and spit you out?"

"I am sure nobody even remembers me. It has been twenty years...twenty years since I was anybody. They have surely moved on with their lives and might not even be in the art world anymore."

"Okay, whatever you say, I am very tired now and want to take a nap. Let me sleep now."

"Okay, mother."

Milo helped his mother to her room and waited for the ambulance. When it arrived, he told the paramedics it was a false alarm and that his mother was feeling better.

After twenty years of obscurity, it was all coming back to him now.

He remembered that first day that he took his art to the streets of Times Square and had made his first hundred dollars. He had come home, and his mother had said, "you get back out there." On the second night a couple bought all his paintings, took him out to dinner, and proposed a toast, "To Milo Sonas, a great artist," they said. And within six months he had his first one man show, and a string of one night events at every happening nightclub in New York. One event took place at a penthouse night club in the center of Times Square called Ecstasy. Its owner was a man from India who never appeared in public. He only spoke to people on the phone. Milo became an "artist in residence" at the club. The man was named Shamon. He arranged for a limo to take Milo to and from his night club. Five hundred FIT and NYU students and trendies waited for the doorman to let them past the velvet ropes. As Milo got out of the limo they all shouted; "Milo! Milo!" The bouncer greeted him with a pat on the back. He rode up the elevator to the top floor. There his paintings were up and big windows showed a breathtaking panoramic view of all of New York City. There was an open champagne bar for an hour. That night he met a young actress, long legs, blonde, drunk, and danced with her till 3:00am. She came home with him in the white limo.

DEAD ARTIST

They made love in the back seat, not realizing that the driver's two way dividing window was rolled down just enough for him to witness everything. The Indian driver watched Milo's ass rise and fall, he could catch glimpses of the girl's small model-like breasts, and Milo's hands grasping for them, and then his lips pressed up against them and the car rattled and shook from their backseat acrobatics.

Some sort of force had all of a sudden beamed down on his life. For soon, he began to make the scene at gallery openings in the East Village and photographers took pictures of Milo as soon as he stepped in the doors.

"What happened to you?" his sixteen year old nephew Donny said to him as they cruised suburban Gold Haven, "You live in a motel in Middle America and spend your afternoons in coffee shops getting free refills."

Milo didn't answer his sometimes obnoxious nephew, instead he turned up a hip-hop song on the radio.

"Check out this rap..." his nephew began to holler out a rhyme:

Milo, you are fat as fuck
and you live in a hotel
and you can't get fucked,
you used to be a famous artist in New York City
and now you're all depressed and you can't get no
titty.

The hyper-kinetic song's rhythm thudded on and Milo laughed and shouted. "Now let me take a verse..."

Donny yelled back, "take it...take it..."

Now Milo began his rap:

You're sixteen and weigh two hundred pounds and about as fat as it gets,

You want to be a baseball star, and play with the
NY Mets
   But the truth is you're just a fat fuck with Tourette's.

Donny was laughing when he came back with:
Mr. Milo Sonas can't rap for shit
and he has to face the fact that his life is shit,
he thinks his New York collector is going to save his
ass,
   but that's because Milo is living in the fucking
past."

Milo, tiring of the game, shot back:
"Hey fuck you kid, who do you think you are,
I'm the one who is hip 'cause I'm driving this car."

And Donny responded:
Your aren't hip, man
you're forty five,
and you just learned how to drive
   and you only get to drive this car while your
mommy is alive."

Milo drove them to the gym where the two played
an extremely loud game of racquetball. Milo and his
rowdy sixteen year old nephew yelled at the top of their
lungs and the sound reverberated in the racket ball
court. They had no regard for what the other gym
members or staff might think. Here was Milo in his
mid-forties still living the life of a teenager. "You get
to be a boy all over again," Dr. Hyatt had said to Milo.
"Lucky you."
   Donny and Milo shared many afternoons together,
they went to the local mall, they lunched at Blimpie's
where Donny would order extravagant sandwiches with
meat balls, bacon and layers of melted cheese. They

went to sushi restaurants together, Donnie's treat. He was a generous kid who stole cash from his parents' wallets.

Donny often bragged about his youthful sexual conquests during these lunches. Milo could not score in Middle America. Milo admired his hyper-kinetic nephew who spewed out obscenity laced raps, scored with women his age, played tournament winning tennis and pitched a mean game of baseball. He was a teenage wonder of testosterone. He was even a ping pong master. And there was a good chance this kid was going to making millions one day in the hot afternoon sun playing that all American game of baseball.

After dropping Donny at his house Milo wondered if all of this was really happening. Was he truly going to be rescued or would he end up like those that wandered the streets and the book stores and loitered away the afternoon, like the old man with dry gray hair who was always fixing or cleaning the thick lenses of his glasses in the local coffee shops? Or the extremely tall bearded and balding man who dressed in Goodwill sweats and rolled cigarettes and conversed with anyone who would listen; openly admitting that he had just been turned loose by the local mental hospital? Milo understood that there was a fine line between an artist with potential and the homeless whose potential had been misspent.

How could it have come to this? Milo's only friends were his rowdy sixteen year old nephew and two dead artists. Milo lived in an "old timers" hotel. This was the station that life had brought him to and he resigned himself to a fate where he was to become a caricature of a towny, a modern day hobo, somebody who lives under the radar, an eccentric who dresses meticulously in second hand clothing. He waited and lived in low class purgatory until his number was called. All this good luck beckoning was just in the nick of time. This was Milo's chance to be something unimaginable to him until now, to be something most people only dream about, he had a real shot at fame. All thanks to Nick.

Milo knew that fame and fortune were knocking at his door when Nick had called him nine months ago and said, "I have been having dreams about you, I see this image of you speaking on the internet, on YouTube, you are giving a commentary on famous artists like Van Gogh and Picasso.....it's a sign."

Already Milo had been living with visitations from these greats, so it was synergistic that the collector had been having these dreams too.

"I think I can make you a household name." After a short pause, Nick went on to say, "But this is not something that is going to happen overnight."

"How long will it take?" Milo asked and then he felt ashamed for seeming impatient.

"Six to nine months," Nick said with certainty. "But, I am awaiting financing."

Death was the gift that facilitated the financing that would soon transport Milo into the stratosphere of fame and fortune.

The story goes that Milo's dealer Nick volunteered to spend time at a senior home where he had befriended an old retired businessman. Nick had shown diligent loyalty to this stranger every Saturday afternoon for five years. When the man died, he willed Nick hundreds of thousands of dollars.

Death was working for Milo.

There had been another agent who had tried to save Milo's career, he was an older local art consultant. They had lunched, but when this man lost his wife to a particularly aggressive form of cancer he did not have the heart to carry on.

Death can be a deterrent or death can be a tool.

"You were once hot shit in New York," Donny said before getting out of the car at his parent's house. "You'll see, you'll get your shit together, we believe in you Uncle Milo."

He was a good kid after all.

But how did it ever come to this?

Milo sometimes indulged in paranoid thoughts. In these fantasies, his dealer would sponsor Milo to create a huge inventory of new works and then promptly kill him and watch the value of the art shoot up.

The prospect of fame and fortune was having a profound effect on his family. His brother Ray simply could not understand how this change of tide had happened right under his nose. Everything, Ray thought, had been as it should be. Milo's failings boosted Ray's ego. Things were so much simpler that way.

Coffee was stronger and bolder with a washed up brother.

The bright sunlight of June was radiant with a marginal brother. A brother on the fringe. A brother on the margin.

Now how would Ray measure his own worth? How could he destroy this? Maybe by helping he could hurt Milo? Perhaps if he could offer bum advice, he could somehow rust what would soon be gold?

When Milo got that call from Ray, it did seem odd; since for all intents and purposes, the brothers had been estranged for years. "I just called to say that I am so sorry for what I said the last time we spoke. I really shouldn't have said that. It was just a plain mean thing to say," Ray said, his voice familiar and grating.

Milo knew exactly what phone call Ray was referring to. It was a few years ago and Milo was telling him how one day, if he could ever get his feet on the ground, he would to move to a big city again like Chicago or New York. Ray had said, "Maybe there are some halfway houses that you could move into."

That cruel comment was like a knife wound in Milo's ribs.

"Listen man," Ray said. "I was just kidding when I said that. The truth is I am really happy for you. But look, I never liked seeing you down and out and living in a hotel. I will be the second happiest person in the world to see you do well. I am just hoping that for your sake this time you know how to hold on to it. I just don't want to see you fuck the whole thing up. Okay, hold on, there I go being harsh again. Sorry."

"Listen, for your information, I didn't fuck anything up."

"Then what happened, how did you lose your whole career?"

"I don't know, I just don't know."

Ray heard Milo's voice break, and it wasn't because the telephone reception was bad, it was because Milo felt like he was about to break down, and cry.

"I feel like I could..." Milo said that night on the phone with Dr. Hyatt.

"Like you could what, Milo?"

"Like I could break."

"You can break but you will never be broken," Dr. Hyatt said.

Chapter Seven

Girls used to track him down in hotel rooms, like the one in Atlantic City. Milo was hired to draw instant brightly colored portraits at a convention. The crowds waited for hours in line to get their turn to be drawn by Milo Sonas. And there he was inhaling the fumes of big fat fluorescent Japanese markers called Sakura. They paid him twenty five hundred dollars for a day's work. Pretty employees of the company accompanied him to lunch. Milo was nervous in front of beauty. Success came at him hard, strong and sensual and he had no manager, no agent then, no collector, no Nick. It all just suddenly happened at him, and he had to navigate his way through the deals, the personalities, the women.

That night in the Atlantic City hotel suite, he tried but failed to wash the fluorescent colors off his fingers. Pink, Blue, Green, Crimson, Pilot marker black.

The phone near his bed rang, and it was a woman's voice on the other end, "Hello, I saw you, what I mean is, I was admiring you. The speed at which you drew. Do you remember me watching? You drew so many people. I hope you don't think I am a stalker calling you like this...but, the company you work for gave me your hotel room number..."

It wasn't long before she was knocking at the door of his hotel room. Okay, she was not a model, but she was lovely, fragile, Latin, youthful, lean, with lithe features that seemed to stretch and grow taller as he looked at her. She was unknown, new. With her he walked the boardwalk, played the slot machines and won some change. When they returned to his hotel room, there were messages from Milo's two best friends wanting to visit him in Atlantic City. "Not a good time," Milo said. The Latin girl was there with him, doing things to him with her soft hands and cold lips.

"Bastardo," Milo said to himself as he thought about his girlfriend back in the city. The first Tina of many Tinas that he would date. This Tina was a blonde Long Island girl, the perfect church going gal, with the perfect middle class family. They didn't like Milo much until he started pulling in a cool ten grand a painting. That family had never seen anything like it. All that eighties-styled money pouring in from of all things, making paintings.

In the arms of this Latin stranger, he thinks about Tina. Oh, Tina the college girl, only eighteen. Milo was twenty six and they'd communicate in high pitched Mickey-Mouse falsettos. Baby talk. "Do you want hand-y?" Tina would ask, "or mouth-y?" Her voice so high, it made him wince.

"I want mouth-y." Milo would squeak back.

"No, just hand-y today....," she would answer. "No mouth-y." And so that's why he was out with other women. Milo wanted mouth-y! He was a naughty boy who wanted lots of mouth-y.

And that is what today's dark-skinned Latin art groupie provided.

All of that had been over twenty years ago. But, it could happen all over again. Nick believed in Milo. And sometimes that is all it takes.

Milo prepared for fame by attending Weight Watchers and running outside. Milo wanted to be beautiful for fame and fortune. He wanted to be the last great crazy artist.

This was his last summer as an unknown.

So it was that after twenty years of toiling, Milo Sonas would become a household name.

All of his life he had survived on favors.

There was his robust young friend Anton who had loaned Milo twenty bucks here, a hundred bucks there through the years. Anton's refrain was, "I know this will all come back to me when you become world famous."

Milo had many a karmic debt to return.

Milo used to be maniacally funny and friends flew him to their weddings to lighten the mood and to add the cache of having at least a formerly happening artist at the festivities. As the nineties droned on, Milo returned to selling on the streets. And watched all his friendships fade away.

Chapter Eight

"When you move back to New York," Pablo said, "you don't have to go to every cocktail party that you are invited to. You should instead focus on creating."

"Let him have his fun," Van Gogh said. "When he goes out he can soak up all that night life and express it in his canvases, as I did."

"You have achieved immortality, yes, you have made your mark. But, in the history books, it always comes back to me, Picasso. There really is nobody else that comes close."

"Okay, you two, cool it," Milo said. "Let's just try to make nice with each other. I am about to start a new life and if you two are going to be going at it all the time, then I won't want you around."

"What about a girl?" Vincent asked. "What about love?"

"What girl? What love?" Milo said.

"There is no girl now for Milo. Milo only dwells in the land of the lonely. He confronts the self, the soul. A woman would only cloud up his view," Pablo insisted. "Anyhow, this guy has lost his ability to get laid, he has lost his touch. He needs lessons from the master."

"Listen to Pablo," said Vincent." He knows of what he speaks."

Milo turned to look at Vincent who was holding Milo's dog Moon, and staring out the window and thinking back upon his desolate, yet creative life. "Yes Milo, don't listen to me, the only women I ever got were women of the night."

"When you want to posses a woman," Pablo said, "you must confront her squarely in the eyes. You must be the Centaur, the beast."

Milo had an answer for that one. "You don't know women these days. Until I am in the bucks, no matter how I confront them, all I am going to do is get a yawn at best. I am over forty, slightly overweight and currently residing in a hotel for people who live on Government checks."

"Well then, "Pablo boomed, "call that goddamn dealer of yours and tell him to get a move on it and to relocate you back to New York, Paris, the French Riviera, anywhere but here in the Midwest."

Milo knew that he could not pressure his dealer. He had learned not to force things in life but instead to let them flow. Something was better than nothing. Time itself would eventually rescue him, as if he were floating on a raft in the turbulent high seas that would one day deliver him to the sands of an enchanted island.

"I'm going out," Milo declared to those two restless passionate greats of modern art who came to visit him and to stay at his apartment and make it feel much more like a home.

He wandered aimlessly, like the last of the disenchanted, a post-bohemian. What if this time it still does not work out? Millions of poor souls live with such let downs. Everything in life does not necessarily pan out. And yet people cope, they don't fall apart, they even put wedding rings on their fingers, they become happy, loving couples. They walk babies in strollers, they maintain their *status quo*. But Milo had sacrificed all of that... the comfort of a body in bed, of a hand holding his hand, of home cooked dinners smoking on the stove. All in the hopes that one day that champagne wave of financial riches might crash over him.

Milo was just grateful to be sleeping at night. He remembered when he could not sleep. He remembered how life hooked him like a cane pulling him off the talent show stage of life. There are people who die from lack of sleep. He could have died!

Milo had only one thing, his talent. Okay so he cracked some jokes and had a way with hitting on young college girls. He used to be able to maintain long term friendships. He remembered his pal Eli. The two of them, buddies for life, drank beer outside a Brazilian nightclub in Copacabana. They sat next to two young hookers who smoked cigarettes and were busy chatting among themselves in the musical language of Portuguese. When he was broke and recovering from clinical depression from a career that tanked, and exhausted from years of the hard sell hustle on 5th Avenue, Astor Place, and Union Square, it was Eli who was his last friend and invited Milo on an all expense paid trip to Rio. They had a couple of women and he had some laughs, but he had no idea where life's tide would take him. The doctors let him go. And Ray told him he was being irresponsible, as usual. Ray told him to grow up and get a life.

Tonight he dreamed his brother Ray took hold of his throat and he desperately tried to pry loose from the strangle hold. Milo awoke to discover Moon resting her head on his neck as she slept. All that commotion had awakened Milo and his dog Moon.

"Whoa, are you okay?" Vincent said. He was sitting on a wooden chair staring past the neon sign to the empty street.

"Oh I just had a wicked nightmare."

"What was it about?"

"I dreamed my brother was strangling me in my sleep."

"You always go on and on about your bad brother, your mean brother. But why don't you ever talk about or think about the good one. The one who sails and sky dives and surfs and hang glides and all that good stuff. That brother to you is like my brother Theo was to me."

"Excuse me, but I need to be alone for a bit."

Milo took Moon out for an after midnight walk.

Chapter Nine

The streets could be tough at this hour and peopled with pimps, crack heads and the homeless, but at least at this hour, the streets almost reminded him of New York at night.

When Milo returned to the hotel lobby he saw that old man again, the one who sat on a wooden church pew and just stared out at the Avenue. He also saw the black cat named Cleo that lived in the lobby and slunk about like a shadow around chairs and tables, and often slept on the ledge of the front window. The hotel was called "The Berkshire" and Milo's monthly rent was a cool twenty five bucks and it would stay that way until Milo got his feet back on the ground. This was government subsidized housing. "Some day," Nick his agent would often say, "this will all just be a bad memory."

Milo was on this way to his second floor studio and the lobby smelled of pot and cigarettes. Up the elevator, through dark halls he walked until he was startled by the sight of a figure standing in the shadows by his door. He stopped for a moment, and Moon gave out a feeble bark. The girl was dressed like a hippie, complete with frayed jeans, a loose fitting tie-dyed T-shirt and colorful scarf wrapped around her fashionably tangled hair. By God it was Samantha, looking even younger than the last time he had seen her which was over seven years ago. As Milo got older his girlfriends seemed to get younger. Samantha had traveled far to be with Milo. How did she find him?

"Mother and father," she said in a drowsy voice because she had been sitting in the dark dank hall so long, "forbade me to visit you here. Father said that he will stop sending me money if I went through with this quest to see you, Milo. He says you aren't ambitious enough. He doesn't think I should be with a street artist."

"How 'bout hello?" Milo said.

"Hi."

"Hi."

They embraced and then Milo whispered into her ear, "I have not been a street artist for years, ever since my last episode."

"My father doesn't want me to be with somebody who has suffered from clinical depression either."

"Then why did you come across the country to see me without even calling first?"

"Because you begged me to come."

"Begged?"

"More like pleaded."

"I don't remember doing that."

She dropped her dufflebag and let her back pack slide off her shoulders and fall on the hallway floor.

"It was during your breakdown."

"Oh, no wonder I don't remember, I don't remember most of what I said during my breakdown. Anyhow, that was five years ago. You're a little bit late. If you would have called then, when I called you, maybe things would have worked out differently."

"You think that if I had come to see you it would have prevented you from your breakdown?"

"It is amazing what getting laid can do for a man." Milo laughed.

"Apparently." Samantha returned his smile.

"What did you come here for?"

"To save you."

46

"Okay."

He inserted his key and opened the front door. They went inside.

"And just how do you intend to save me?"

"By giving you hope," she said.

"I think you came here because you got wind of all the good shit that is going down for me now."

"A man with potential is only viable when he is under thirty five, after that it just seems creepy if he still has hope. At this point in your life, you have to already be there, you have to already have arrived to impress a woman. I didn't get on a Greyhound bus to watch the rest of you wither away."

"So I take it you are not impressed by the prospect of my becoming a world class artist."

"No."

"Then I will ask you one more time, why did you come?"

"Because I am a sexy dumb twenty-six year old who doesn't know what the fuck she is doing."

"So you're twenty-six now."

"Yep. Nobody stays nineteen forever.'

"Would you like a beer?"

"Sure"

"The fact that you would get on a Greyhound bus and travel for two and a half days to see me, for me, is an omen that things are starting to happen."

"Yes, I have suffered to see you again. In the past two days, on that nasty bus I have heard a baby cry for eight hours, I have heard the sound of retching vomit and I had the honor of sitting in the only available seat next to the toilet. Oh yeah and I also saw a couple, I think they were trailer park newlyweds, anyhow they were getting it on in their seat. They get kudos for ingenuity, as she straddled him, she looked directly into my eyes, as if to dare me to tell the bus driver what was happening. The rest of the passengers were asleep....it was sexy scary, if you know what I mean."

"All this, you went through just to see me."

"Just to see you."

"You know Greyhound is running a special, two can travel round trip for the price of one, that means I have one free return ticket. Do you want to come back to New York with me? Waddayou say?"

Milo wanted nothing more, but he couldn't just leave now, not while his mother was in critical condition, not now while all his family was flying out to Gold Haven just to see her one last time. These were the last loose ends that he had to tie up. The least he could do was to stay for the end of an era. The era of his smothering, loving, cruel and wonderful mother.

Milo said, "My agent, Nick, said that he will send for me in the fall, this is my last summer here in Gold Haven."

Before they headed out into the night, Samantha and Milo jumped right back into their former pattern -- they instantaneously threw off their clothing, and wildly attempted to make love and Milo was reminded of why it was that the two of them broke up in the first place. Sure enough Samantha still had that condition where her vagina constricted during intercourse making it nearly impossible, and certainly cumbersome for a penis to penetrate her, even if she was willing. And so the fucking became a slapstick endeavor in which Milo would try to slip inside her while his erection lasted and she invariably would clamp her thighs, shutting him out. Milo would then attempt to gently but firmly pry her legs back open, and she would unwillingly resist. Making love to her was like trying to open a giant resistant mussel at a seafood restaurant. It was frightfully unsexy and finally during the wrestling match Milo would lose his erection and Samantha would eagerly perform fellatio and when he was hard again they would resume the process. This X-rated sitcom pattern would repeat over and over again, but to no avail, and she would end up offering to finish him off with her weepy lips or her nervous hands as she apologized for her physiological hang-up, assuring him all the while that she really wanted to, but that she could not due to her involuntary inner muscular psycho sexual contraction.

Tonight Milo passed on her offer for a sexual favor as a form of completion, he was too flustered to enjoy.

Instead they ate Chinese at a fast food joint called Ming Garden which was just about to close when they arrived. The two shared General Tsao chicken, Coke, tea, and let the atonal twang of Chinese pop music temporarily wash away the reminder of why it was they just might not be meant to be.

"What I just witnessed was total embarrassment." Pablo said later that night as Samantha slept.

Milo was up, drawing in a sketch pad by the window.

"First of all, you should not have been watching me, number two, don't blame me. And you can't blame her either. I really don't want to talk about it."

"Of course I am going to blame you," Pablo was smoking a cigarette and clouding up the room. "It's up to you to relax her and to properly seduce her."

"I did, I tried. You saw me, no matter how long I spend on foreplay the same thing always happens."

"I still think you could be more patient. The girl loves you, why don't you marry her. Marriage can be very useful to a man. Did you know those were my last words?"

"How can I marry her? I don't feel ready."

"You are ready. Marry her, and you will see things begin to happen. I promise you that."

"I will think about it, Pablo."

Chapter Ten

"It's me."

It was Luna.

"What's up?" Milo said.

"Mother's in the hospital."

"What happened?

"She was having heart palpitations."

"I'll be right there."

Mrs. Sonas shared a hospital room with another old lady, and she was not happy about it. All that Sonia Sonas wanted was to be home. "Let me die at home," she kept repeating, her entreaties ignored. "It's enough that I have to die in the Midwest. But I refuse to let myself die with a withering old roommate next to me. Also I refuse to die until I get to see success return to your life, Milo. Besides you owe me... money." She said this halfheartedly, "Thirty five thousand dollars, that's the exact amount. Remember you promised me you would pay your old mother back."

Milo remembered and nodded obediently. Truth is, he never really thought that the day would actually materialize when he could repay his mother for all she had done.

She would not relent. She said, with gravelly voice, "In a drawer, in my room, on the cabinet next to the TV set, I have the financial records...go take a look at them if you want."

"I am sure that Milo will be happy to repay you for all you have done," Luna said. "So you better stay healthy for us, so that you can get all those dollar bills!"

Mrs. Sonas smiled for she said all these things in cloying jest. But Milo knew deep down she meant every last word, and expected back every last penny. She loved her son, but a debt was a debt.

"Mother, this is Samantha, from New York," Milo said, changing the subject. "She was the girl that I was dating during 9/11. Remember the one who never quite made it out to your Thanksgiving that year."

"Hey," Sonia Sonas said. "You owe me too. I paid for that plane ticket, the one you never took. It's okay dear, I forgive you."

"I am sorry about that. I truly am, I just couldn't wake up that morning."

"I tried and tried to wake you, to catch the flight but you just wouldn't get the hell up." Milo said to Samantha.

"Can we not go into this right now?" Samantha put her finger on Milo's lips, silencing him.

"Do me this one last favor," his mother said, "Go to the house and read the files, and you will see, Milo you owe me. Please go there now."

"Okay, we will. Don't worry, I promise to repay you. I do."

After their awkward visit with his mother, Milo and Samantha had some coffee in the hospital diner. Milo had a thing for hospital diners, it was fun and comforting to dine with doctors, nurses, orderlies, all in blues and whites. One could feel their camaraderie. This diner had a low ceiling, and served mashed potatoes and meat loaf, and featured an unspectacular salad bar.

They took a taxi to Mrs. Sonas's house. Milo let himself in with his key, and in her chilly basement office area he found his mother's journal and sure enough there were all the records. He randomly flipped through the handwritten accounts:

DEAD ARTIST

Breakfast with Milo. $14.99 1999

Gallon of white acrylic paint purchased at Pearl paint. $80 1991

$550 rent for October 1991

$550 rent for December 2000

Milo told Samantha that reading these meticulous and obsessive accounts got him down. So Milo and Samantha walked to East Town where they ordered some latte from a thriving little locally-owned coffee shop, and strolled down the mostly empty streets.

"Why now Mother, must you do this... this summer on the cusp of everything opening up for me?" Milo railed.

A striking young mother dressed in sheer white summer Gap pants held hands with her husband as their child wandered ahead.

A barber shop was broadcasting soft rock from tiny outdoor speakers, the music carried by hot summer breezes. As they walked, it occurred to Milo that Samantha surely looked like his college-aged daughter with her hair still wet from a morning shower. Her thick mane of hair took forever to dry. Usually it didn't dry until night.

Of all the times to start dying, why now?

June was for weddings, for outdoor rock concerts and for landscape painters like Vincent who they spotted standing with his easel on Main Street, painting the one outdoor cafe in town. And summer was for the skateboard kids that playfully circled Vincent, and for the town schizophrenic dressed in sweats with thick blue winter socks and a dress shirt. He spent his days at that cafe rolling his own cigarettes and taking advantage of the coffee refill policy, which was bottomless.

Vincent winked at Milo as he, with loaded paint brush created his thick impasto vision of the cafe. The iron chairs, the banister, the big window, the schizophrenic at his table. All of this on the canvas looked twisted, tortured and vibrating with color intensity. Vincent took a boring afternoon scene and made it buzz.

"There is somebody that I would like you to meet," Milo said escorting Samantha by the arm in a gentlemanly fashion from the Cafe across Main Street to where the world famous painter was busy dashing, and almost whipping the canvas with his brush.

"Samantha this is Vincent Van Gogh. Vincent this is Samantha Tristan."

Vincent looked at Milo like he was out of his mind -- introducing a girlfriend to him. She will never see me, thought Vincent and then she will turn against Milo and he will lose her. People don't see the world the way Milo does. And now this Pace University student, who skipped class to sleep in on the morning of 9/11, this lovely lucky girl will just think you are plain crazy. Don't self sabotage your love, Milo! Vincent's eyes widened and seemed to radiate the message, "Don't do it!"

But Milo with his new found confidence just didn't care.

"Hi," Samantha said unaffectedly, with her natural likability.

Vincent was so taken aback with surprise that somebody else besides Milo could actually see him, that he let the yellow soaked brush fall out of his hand. It landed on the sidewalk looking like scrambled eggs. With his hand now brush-less, he extended it and shook her small warm hands. Samantha stepped forward and accidentally stepped into the paint. She was wearing only flip flops and her orange painted toe nails were now blending yellow.

"Whoops," he said.

DEAD ARTIST

"It's cool," said Samantha. "How many girls get to have a pedicure from...well, from the father of modern art. But then again, you look too young to be a father."

"She's fun," he said to Milo, allowing himself to smile even though inside there was a hollowness.

"Yes, she can be very funny."

Milo was thinking back to the Cirque du Soleil-like contortions of their attempts at love making the night before.

Will they ever be able to consummate? Was Pablo right? Should Milo go ahead and marry this simple, kind, loyal Polish girl who majored in photography and who he had not seen in seven years? That is, not until last night. It was true they had a bond -- they shared one of the pivotal moments in modern history. Samantha and Milo were dating on 9/11.

Samantha examined Vincent's richly textured painting. "You're doing a great job of capturing the mood of this afternoon. I wish I could paint like the two of you. You guys are so lucky. All I can do is take pictures, that is nothing compared to what you both do. Let me get a shot of you two."

Samantha had her digital camera hanging like a pendant from her neck. She pulled it over her head, and aimed the tiny high tech camera at Vincent who stood humbly and nervously next to Milo. She checked her view finder to see the image she had just taken. The review image showed Milo standing alone. There was no sign of Vincent or the easel or Vincent's painting of the East Town cafe. But she didn't react, or call attention to what she now understood. She knew now that it was impossible for Vincent to appear in a photograph but she didn't let on. Why ruin a precious moment?

"May I see the picture?" Vincent asked sheepishly.

"I want to surprise you later, when I Photoshop it, if you don't mind."

"Oh, okay, I understand."

Van Gogh took the canvas off the easel, folded the stand, and the three of them crossed the street to share a cup of coffee at the Cafe. The easel was the kind that could store all the oil paint in a wooden drawer. Milo never thought he would see the day when he would sit in an outdoor Cafe in Gold Haven Michigan with Vincent Van Gogh and his hippie-like ex-girlfriend, Samantha.

Samantha didn't waste any time in asking what this was all about. "How is this all possible? What are you doing here Vincent?" she asked, and waited for an answer.

Vincent confessed to her that he was back walking the earth mostly out of anger. He was peeved that things didn't work out in his lifetime and when he got wind of Milo's up and coming re-emergence, Pablo and he agreed that it might be beneficial to hang around Milo to see that he got it right. "We just don't want Milo to blow it."

Vincent poured so much sugar in his espresso that one could see a white island in the black sea of the cup, that is until the island sank. He said, "We had been watching as Milo diligently worked the streets of New York all those afternoons and evenings. Milo was willing to hustle his wares and play lotto with life all in the hope that one day he would strike it lucky. It was really touching and we all agreed that, you Milo, should be the one who would blow the roof off of what could be accomplished by an artist during his lifetime. You're going to blow up boy. Do it for me, you hear?" Vincent was coining a hip-hop phrase. He was in touch.

The three of them laughed together and then Vincent's mood suddenly dropped. He excused himself, stood up and looked directly into the sun. Then, he stepped into the street, which was blazing and bright, and dematerialized, easel under his arm.

Samantha had a deep compassion for others, especially older men. She did not make any mention of his ghostly disappearance. She had observed Vincent's demeanor closely though, and said, "Did you notice how he became suddenly despondent?"

"He is always that way."

"No it is more than that, it seems to me like he has what is called "low affect." I learned about it in a psych class, it's when a person is unable to express a full range of emotion. Usually it is the residue of a mental breakdown or of medication. To me Vincent came off as clinically depressed, possibly on a downward spiral."

"Okay, so, what's new. Van Gogh has a mood disorder. Go figure."

"But," Samantha said, smiling, "they have medications for that. There are treatments."

"Are you saying Van Gogh needs to take meds?"

"Why not? It might help him bring down the intensity of his condition just one notch."

"Look! Can you blame him for getting depressed? People are making millions off of his art and he is dead and there is nothing he can do about it but sit back and watch."

"But he believes in you Milo."

"It would seem that way."

"Doesn't that make you happy?"

"Okay, so a couple of dead artists believe in me. What good is that going to do me?"

"You should be flattered."

"Okay, so I am flattered."

"I wish I was granted other worldly visitations. You see Milo, you have a charmed life."

She gave him a peck on the cheek and he felt again the comfort that she had offered him so many years ago.

Chapter Eleven

You were an art world soldier in your street days, living on rations of beans and rice during the cold harsh winter. You wore combat boots and brought out your own canteen of water and a thermos of black coffee. You wore thermal underwear and thick socks. You had a "stone-cold" no-frills sales tactic, only answering customers' questions pertaining directly to your art. You didn't divulge one iota about your education or training and didn't allow customers to talk about other living artists when they came to your makeshift aluminum table with your paintings leaning against it. You sold on the street seven days a week from 3:00pm until 6:00pm, and never deviated from these hours, even on New Years Day, 3:00pm to 6:00pm, as always, and the results were that within this three hour window your sales increased several-fold within one year.

Milo's hard core guerrilla tactics worked. One hot summer night, a group of well-dressed Beverly Hills tourists approached Milo's table and said: "Tell us, what *is* the story behind this painting of the bearded man?"

Coldly, Milo responded. "Could you step away from the paintings, please," expecting them to walk away. But, while the finely dressed ladies may have been taken aback by his firm tone, the seriousness of his tone intrigued one of the rich housewives.

She persisted, and asked again, "So what is the *meaning* of this painting?"

Milo answered. "The explanation behind that painting is reserved for the person that purchases the painting. If I were to tell you the meaning behind that painting and you didn't buy it, then you would bring me bad Karma."

Within twenty minutes, and an explanation the buyer may not have understood, Milo closed on twelve hundred dollars worth of art. With that, Milo learned that by being proprietary about his art he could bring up the prices for each piece.

Milo answered his cell phone on the fourth ring. "Ola, Milo, dis is Consuelo." Consuelo was the twenty-four hour duty nurse who watched over his mother after her release from the hospital. She had a thick accent and high pitched chirp of a voice and with her primitive Spanglish, she was barely communicative. She was a Costa Rican girl who was painfully shy and short, but glowed emotionally ever since she had met her fiancee who washed dishes at a nearby Mexican restaurant called La Cantina. Consuelo would soon be married, but had to conceal her joy because these were solemn times indeed for Doña Sonia who was fading away into delirium and oblivion.

"Your madre, emergencia. You come to casa quickly."

When the taxi pulled up at the house, Consuelo was in her loose fitting nurse's uniform standing on the front lawn. There was a ladder leaning against the front of the house and Consuelo was gesturing and pointing upward. After paying the cabbie, Milo positioned himself in the center of the lawn. He looked like he was saluting but he was only shielding his eyes from the glaring sun so he could witness what had worked Consuelo up so.

DEAD ARTIST

Sonia Sonas was at the top of the ladder, in a free flowing flannel night gown holding a small shovel in her hand.

"What are you doing up there?" Milo yelled up to his mother.

Milo found this vision harder to believe than his visions of Picasso and Van Gogh. His mother had been bedridden for weeks and yet, there she was, at the top of a ladder in the summer sun. Had she gone mad? Was she dead, and just visiting?

"Oh, hello Milo. Beautiful day, no? A wonderful day to clean the gutters."

Clean the gutters? He could not wrap his mind around what he was seeing. She was dying. It was the sunset of her life, the end of her era.

He called out to her, "You know I promised to help you out with the gutters. You aren't supposed to be up there. Must I remind you that you are 79 years old and that if you fall off that ladder you could break your bones and old, brittle bones don't heal. What if you broke your hip? I have heard about terrible things happening to old people when they break their hips."

Was he really having this conversation?

"If you call me an old person one more time, I am going to sock you one. I don't like labels. Not today or any day. Can't you see that this afternoon I feel forty?"

It seemed his mother was experiencing a second wind.

"Por favor," Consuelo said, her voice barely audible with the sound of the passing traffic on the street. "Dona Sonia, please come down, por favor."

Sonia dug out some decayed leaves and tossed them playfully at her son. "These gutters must be cleaned before the next big rainfall." She scooped up more dirt and flung it freely into the wind.

"Your mother is a real stinker." Samantha said, gently stroking Milo's back. And now the three of them, Consuelo, Samantha and Milo couldn't keep from breaking into contagious laughter.

Chapter Twelve

"We have never seen this sort of thing happen," Dr. Basil said to Milo. "Your mother has an irregular heart beat, and congestive heart failure. She has swelling and water retention in her joints, and prior to this spontaneous recovery our recommendation was for you to transfer her to hospice care. Now our diagnosis has changed, and we can only take a wait-and-see approach. All I can say is please try to keep your mother off the roof, for God's sake."

"Thank you, Doctor."

Milo's private counsel with the doctor was complete with that exchange, and he returned to the waiting room where his mother was filling up on the hospitality decaf.

As she sugared up her coffee she said to Milo, "What I can't understand is that you seem disappointed that I am better. It is as if you wanted me to die or something."

"No Mother, I don't want you to die...but I will admit I was resigning myself to that very real inevitability."

"I have spontaneously recovered due to all that is happening for you. And you deserve it after all you have been through, honey. That's why I'm still here -- for you."

During the taxi ride home from the hospital there was total silence.

On the streets of New York City Milo chased a dream of immortality. Each time he made a painting he was freeze drying a moment. Frozen moments are everlasting. While people are reluctant to surrender two hours to a movie, there will always be people who will stand in line outside a museum just for the chance of walking by the soundless works on canvas, or the mute creations made of wood or steel or marble. And the tired, yet eager tourists from around the world will line up year round to crane their necks upward to witness Michelangelo's "orgy like" ode to flesh, gesture and muscle which is the Sistine Chapel. You would think by the long lines that this was the opening of a Harry Potter movie, but no, it is for Michelangelo, Picasso and Van Gogh that they wait and will continue to wait to see their art. Clusters of people queue around the bullet proof shrine that is the Mona Lisa, just to catch a glimpse of her monochrome mystery. These works will always be relevant to those that travel and those that just wander in the afternoons.

Chapter Thirteen

Your nervous crack up really knocked you out of the art game. And, your complete disappearance from the New York scene made your artwork rise in value. Your last day selling on the street in Union Square was most memorable. You sold a painting of Vincent Van Gogh for three hundred bucks, cash, and you knew in your heart that it was the end of your era. You knew that any day the paintings would show your weariness. You couldn't go on without sleep.

Milo had forgotten how to sleep. And yet, he never tired. After the quick sale on Union Square he rolled up his cart of paintings and stopped in Union Square Park. Looking around him, he saw others like himself lying in the grass. He saw lovers, and he saw single people just lying down in the afternoon. He realized he had never let himself rest, not for twenty years. So he found a spot and a patch of grass, and he positioned himself on the ground and looked up at the sky. He simply could not go on. He closed his eyes but could not sleep. After maybe twenty minutes he got up again and returned to his urban cave where he poured the colors onto the plates, and began another rather muted portrait of Vincent. Always Vincent. He was obsessed with Vincent, and the street crowds from all walks of life loved his versions of the Dutch master, that crazy shaman. But this last painting of Vincent he could not finish.

Mid-painting, Milo found that he could not hold the brush any longer, and he let it drop into the plate of white paint. He could not go on this way. He was now a casualty of New York. A victim of his own hopes and ambitions. He had become someone who wandered in the afternoon, and then he collapsed.

A good friend of Milo was an expatriate and happened to be in town. He came to visit that evening. When Milo saw him, he embraced him tightly, as if he were Milo's brother. The good one. But he was not good-brother Paul, nor was he bad-brother Ray, his name was Eli, and he had been Milo's best friend, prior to the time when he had left New York to live in Copacabana.

All of Milo's friends had bailed out of New York City, and self-absorbed Milo suddenly realized that he missed them. Eli thought it strange that he was so touchy-feely with him. He confessed to Eli that his family beckoned, and that his mother wanted him to come home to the Midwest, to rest.

"Please help me," Milo pleaded. "I don't want to spend one more day in this room."

"Of course," he said with a thick Israeli accent, that sounded like the words first swam in his saliva before leaving his mouth. "I understand Milo. If I had to live in this dump for even a week, I would commit suicide. I'll get you out of here."

"Thanks, that's just what I needed to hear." Milo quickly fell asleep while Eli stood over him.

Eli took care of all the details, he could always be counted on to make arrangements, it was what he did best.

This is how it happened, Milo's deliverance into the delusional dream of a nervous breakdown. At least, this is how Milo remembers it happening.

Eli arranged for Milo to spend the night at a mutual friend who owned a French restaurant and a Bed and Breakfast on City Island. But first he was escorted to an Upper East Side cocktail party. His friends, at least the ones he recognized, tried to keep him occupied and entertained and well fed so that he could avoid recurring panic attacks. The condo had a balcony view of Park Avenue, and at times during the evening, Milo found himself unsure of how he was transported from his cellar squalor to Upper East Side luxury. Mr. Handsome Host lived in a comfortable if not slightly sanitized environment, and seemed to be married. His wife, a gentle, and clearly well-kept hostess quietly informed guests that Milo was "not well."

"I am fine," Milo insisted, "I want to have a drink. Something hard."

Mrs. Handsome served Milo a dirty Martini, not denying him his right to a good stiff drink. After downing the martini, Milo stepped out onto the high-rise balcony and announced, "I have changed my mind, I don't want to leave New York City in the morning."

Mr. Handsome, looked first at Milo, then the balcony rail, then over the side. With his male model stubble reflecting in the moonlight, he spoke firmly, "Milo, let me ask you a question." He paused, waiting for Milo to make eye contact, and said, "Are you happy?" He smelled of cologne.

"Who cares if I am happy?" Milo seemed to move closer to the balcony rail and raised his voice. "I don't want to go."

"That's good, Milo. But, think about it -- are you happy?"

Milo stood silently. His mind was rushing, thinking of all the sidewalks down below where he had sold his canvases. He thought about Columbus Avenue, West Broadway, Fifth and Sixth Avenues, Astor Place, he thought about sales made after midnight in front of the Virgin Megastore downtown on Broadway. And he thought about setting up shop in front of movie houses, closing deals when the films let out. And, all the beautiful girls he had sold to, handsome gay couples, wealthy power couples, black and white, Asian and Hispanic. Milo had sold to collectors from Beirut to Delhi to Rome, and was very popular with Japanese tourists and the wealthy ladies of Spain.

Milo felt dizzy and closed his eyes. Mr. Handsome took two steps closer to Milo and eyed the balcony rail, now within Milo's reach.

That life, that primitive bohemian outgoing outdoor life in which all he had to do was roll his cart full of color drenched paintings, set up his table, take a seat in his canvas director chair and catch the cash that seemed to fall from the city trees, and then roll on home (often with some Lolita-like university coed girl in tow) or perhaps he rolled his cart home alone, just wearing head phones and listening to WBLS play retro R and B. In his mind, he looked back and it was all so magical, those afternoons of handing out business cards systematically to a dozen select women a day, playing the numbers game and then from that effort would come the messages on the phone from female voices. When the girls come calling, then you really have something they want. Yet for all his sexual conquests there were also spectacular failures.

Time seemed to slow, and Milo shifted his weight.

He had been stood up so many times he could be listed in the Guinness book of records. Eli used to say with his impasto Israeli accent, "You Milo are a tortured soul. You wait for these women to arrive, rearranging your studio, scrubbing, mopping, buying cheap beer, chips and tequila. Why do you do it?" And, he did it on a 99 cent shop budget. Milo could wine and dine women from the confines of his cave-like studio at a fraction of the cost most bachelors spent.

"Milo?" Mr. Handsome called.

DEAD ARTIST

He stood at the balcony rail and a crowd formed at the terrace doors. He looked over at worried faces, and looked through the confused looks on what seemed like total strangers. His mind returned to the streets, and his other famous hunting grounds – the Met and Barnes and Noble. The bookstore was a nightclub, tall skim lattes were the liquor, and the whole place was just a singles mixer without name tags. Milo brazenly struck up conversations in Barnes and Noble, trawling the place for single women. One he had snared told him her name was Cleopatra, and claimed it was her birth name. Milo didn't believe it. He didn't care. He listened while she said she was looking for work, and that she might take up work at a new gallery in Chelsea. Great, something in common. He gave her his card and moved on. The rule is, they must call him.

And she did, that same night. She came to his cave, ate his spicy beans and rice, drank his Shlitz beer from the can, did some tequila shots, and devoured his salad. They had apple sauce for desert, and Milo air popped popcorn. Puffed kernels shot into the air like Fourth of July fireworks and he wasn't going to bother to sweep them up. It made the kitchen festive, and he was celebrating the conquest of a beautiful girl. It didn't take long for them to get drunk and start feeling good. She told him sexy risqué stories, and then later as they sat close she took them all back and claimed none of them were true. Confused, but already having made the investment in her, Milo went for the kiss and she said "*she doesn't feel it*", and that this "*was not enough for her.*" But she said, "I can be your girlfriend for fifty dollars an hour." She'd even sleep over, but not in his bed.

This didn't fit Milo's budget, but he was drunk and there was a fifty in his wallet. In one hour she did everything to him and nothing for him, because that

69

wasn't what he wanted. All he really wanted was, was...something else.

"Are you happy?" The worried host of Milo's last cocktail party in Manhattan asked again and again.

And then, Milo found he couldn't stop the tears and said, simply, "No."

That's all he could remember.

It was time for New York to spit you out.

So Milo left New York for Michigan to have his nervous breakdown elsewhere.

Nick was always reminding Milo that, "Leaving New York, disappearing and getting off the streets was the best thing that ever happened to your artistic career. It gave you all the artistic advantages of dying, without the downside. Things always happen for a reason."

Milo lived with constant paranoia as he created an extensive inventory of new canvases. Would Nick kill him off so that he could market a trove of works by a dead artist?

Milo Sonas. Dead artist.

Maybe Milo was a bit obsessed with death during this peculiar time when his mother kept dying and coming back to life. He never knew if he was mourning her imminent death or rejoicing her rebounding health.

It was a time of great duality. He seemed to have two things happening simultaneously. Here he was on the cusp of a major career re-emergence, a chance to be world renowned, but at the same time his mother was in terrible shape. He had heard people say that tending to somebody who is dying could actually be a beautiful, memorable experience. He had read about one middle aged woman who found that tending to her grandmother's death was so touching that she decided to seek work at a hospice after her grandmother's passing. She just couldn't get enough of it.

DEAD ARTIST

Milo found his mother's imminent death to be like an anchor tugging him down into an abyss.

Chapter Fourteen

"I think I understand now why you came here," Milo said. Samantha was in the bathtub.

He knew it was because they had been through 9/11 together. Prior to the moment when the planes hit the Towers, they had been drifting apart as lovers. But as soon as it happened, as soon as he saw the footage on TV, and then looked outside his door and saw the people heading up Second Avenue covered in white dust, that is when he called her and pleaded with her to be with him. And he still believed that her subsequent availability was the luckiest thing that ever happened to him. The phenomena of having a girlfriend, somebody in his life during that hellish historic time prolonged his psyche's survival.

His phone call had awakened her, and she was still groggy when he said: "Two planes have just hit the Twin Towers. Come to me, please come to me, I think it's war, and if it's the end of the world I want you here with me."

He stepped outside with his cell phone, and he saw his tall lanky neighbor who was a dead ringer for Kramer in Seinfeld. And instantly their long standing grudge disappeared and they shook hands. His neighbor was a real "Hey Joe" character and swore, "I will personally beat the shit out of whomever is responsible for hitting those Towers."

Samantha took the subway from Queens and made it to Milo's cave before the City cut subway service. That afternoon, thinking it might be the end of the world, they made love and miraculously that day her psycho-sexual condition subsided and her body accepted him. They came together like patriotic clashes of chimes. She joined him on September 12th when he had no choice but to get back to work and sell his art on Union Square, though he felt like he shouldn't have gone out to the streets out of respect for the victims. But he was broke and he had no choice. He sold a painting of Lady Liberty on 9/12 for three hundred and fifty dollars, and the customer blessed him. In September of 2001, he symbolized one of the things that made New York City great – genuine hard-working street artists.

As he rolled home from that sale he ran into an art world acquaintance who also blessed him. The man was a journalist for an obscure downtown periodical and they chatted for a bit. This man told Milo that he knew of an artist who had won a competition to have a studio set up in the Twin Towers, and that the artist had chosen to spend the night in his studio. He was there when the Towers fell. As the writer spoke, Milo suddenly recalled that he had also entered that World Trade Center art competition. When Milo got back to his place he searched through his filing cabinets and found the application to that foundation, it was filled out but never sent.

With night came thunder above the great city. Samantha and Milo couldn't help but think that New York was being bombed.

And ashes filled the air like a macabre Christmas snow and Milo had to wear a tee shirt tied like a bandana around his mouth when he went out to pick up some items from the Korean grocer on the corner. Those first few days it seemed as though all of New York was suffering together from a collective neurosis. Milo had canceled his appointment with Dr. Hyatt that week because the doctor was on the eleventh floor and because he didn't want to ride in an elevator. It also seemed as though the world had fallen in love with New York all over again, just as Milo fell back in love with Samantha. Milo's family had called trying to convince him to take a train to the Midwest, but Milo couldn't bring himself to leave the drama, the love making, the feeling of camaraderie on the streets, the street selling, the city, the strangely exhilarating feeling of survival in a time of doom.

It seemed Samantha was waiting for Milo to do something, to make his move, perhaps to propose. He never did. And so when Thanksgiving came, she unconsciously took revenge on him by refusing to get out of bed and catch the flight with him to Gold Haven.

And now, seven years later, Samantha said to him, "We shared 9/11 together, and I have come to see you now. Some people can say we will always have Paris. But we can say we will always have 9/11. And even though, in so many ways, it was a terrible time, in some ways, I am ashamed to say it, it was the most wonderful time of my life. Because it brought everyone together, including us."

They both remembered how for a time it seemed that everybody in the city loved each other.

Milo reminded Samantha that she stood him up on that, oh so important Thanksgiving after the attacks.

"My father didn't want me to continue seeing you. He said you weren't ambitious enough and that he wouldn't support me if I kept seeing you. I'm sorry." She paused and looked to him for a reaction. "And then I heard you left New York City. Why did you leave?"

"I just didn't want to live the rest of my life in that cave."

"I understand."

"Plus as you know I had a pretty bad nervous breakdown."

"I'm sorry."

"It's okay now, there is a happy ending. And old collector of mine, he believes in me. His name is Nick."

"Sometimes it only takes one person to make a difference."

"Samantha will you stay here, until my mother is gone?"

"Yes of course I will, no matter how long it takes."

"Well, it's not like we are rushing her, she will go when she is ready to go." Milo smiled.

"And more than that, I want to help Vincent out as well. I sense he is as lonely as you are. There is a friend of mine, I'll call her. I just know they would hit it off. She doesn't have much happening in her life right now and she is just the type to do something spontaneous. And I hope she will be able to actually see Vincent, like I can. Somehow I know he will be visible to her."

"You are the only person that I know that has been able to see Vincent."

"She will be able to, I just know it."

Chapter Fifteen

What so amazed Milo was how his mother lost interest in food and water, yet her biological mechanisms seemed to sustain themselves, waiting for each member of the family to fly out to Gold Haven to see her one last time.

And, in contrast to Sonia's dwindling health, Milo and Samantha were rekindling their post-9/11 romance.

Samantha was a simple girl, she loved jangling new rock bands that were rough around the edges, she loved boys who sang with high voices, she especially loved when they screamed and hyperventilated into microphones. She wore jeans with frayed ends that dragged on the ground picking up dust and dirt and grime. And so far, during her visit, she had yet to wear shoes, instead she either went barefoot or wore flip flops.

Samantha called her friend but found that convincing a New York girl to come out to Gold Haven, Michigan was a hard sell. Her friend was living footloose in Brooklyn. When Samantha got off the phone with her friend she said to Milo, "She says she doesn't want to come to some square bible belt community at this juncture in her life. And she said she certainly doesn't want to hang out with some poor artist named Vincent. I didn't tell her who he really was. I wanted to surprise her when she came out. I will try her again later."

Vincent was in the hotel room when she relayed this discouraging information. He was in a particularly testy mood having gone online to the Sotheby's web site where he once again saw the astronomical prices that contemporary art was selling for, and this was art made by living artists. And it certainly didn't make him feel any better to see his paintings sell for tens of millions. He complained that he was born in the wrong century, he hated being a redhead, and he was bummed that he was spending eternity watching actors like Kirk Douglas or Jacques Dutronc play him with such annoying mannerisms.

"What you need is the same thing you have always needed, and that is to get laid." Samantha said.

"A lot of good that will do me now."

She continued, "And more than that, you need to be loved, and I know just the right girl for you. It will just take some coaxing to get her out here. But don't worry, I will do it."

Milo noticed Vincent was nodding off, he was falling in and out of consciousness, "I don't think Vincent is listening. He has not been sleeping well. He has developed a sleeping disorder, and if he continues I will have to take him to a crisis intervention."

"Wait, before you do that let me see if I can convince my girlfriend to come and then everything will be alright. We have the chance here to change the course of history and make Vincent Van Gogh happy."

Milo's troubles were mounting. He was running out of money and it was time to tell his dealer that he needed an advance against future sales.

Milo always ran through the money his dealers gave him. He spent it on frivolous CDs. New running shoes. Trips to the movies with Picasso (Van Gogh took no interest in the movies). Pablo was visible to the ticket takers so Milo had to pay for him, and all the movie tickets, even if they were for matinees, were setting Milo back financially. Pablo found it humorous how

Milo worried about money. "There is no such thing as money in the sixth dimension," he'd say.

Yes, the money was all spent.

He spent the last of it on a particularly stimulating massage at a local Nail Salon called Shangri-La from a rather attractive twenty-something Asian masseuse. "Do you have a girlfriend?" she asked while slowly massaging his buttocks. "No," he said, and then followed her direction to turn over. Then, she serviced him with a surprise.

No, this was not a good time to go broke, not now, with Samantha visiting? Of course, there is seldom a good time for having no money. But, her visit was totally unexpected. Milo never seemed to achieve balance. Sometimes he would have love and sex but no money. And other times he would have lots of cash and nobody to spend it on. It was like his art. There were times when he would roll out his cart and sell out in minutes, and other times (like one terrible August) when he was unable to even give his paintings away. "When would life be orderly?" Milo wondered. Love, affection, bank account, home... so much was pending on the business savvy and know-how of Nick.

And, yes, it was wonderful that he was now signed exclusively to a sales agent. But money wasn't flowing yet. And it was times like these that he wished for his former street selling days, quick cash, in and out. It was now six o'clock. Samantha was sleeping, and it would have been a perfect time to roll out to the good ole Cooper Square and bask in the mad rush of the after-work crowd as they got off the subway and headed home. Oh, but to witness the blur of personhood and the pattern of certain repeating faces. There were those who used to greet him, and those that didn't. He remembered the long legged woman who was a professional dog walker as she walked five dogs from a single lead. There were the flirting NYU and Cooper Union students. And often he would see ex-girlfriends or one-time lovers pass. And if he ever had anything on his mind or if he just wanted to vent, Milo would approach total strangers for free talk therapy. Milo had a keen intuition about strangers and he could always find somebody to talk to -- a fellow vendor, a security guard or a young woman with time to spare. Mostly young women. Oh the street days!

"You know what I think?" Samantha said. It was the middle of the night and Milo's eyes were wide open and pondering. "I think that you are painfully, excruciatingly lonely. And I think that is why Pablo and Vincent visit you. It's as if you are beyond having any friends in the real world. It's like you had to reach to another dimension for camaraderie. But I'm here now, Milo and everything is going to be all right. And Vincent, if you are in this room, hearing me, even though I can't see you at this moment, listen, everything is going to be all right for you too."

Samantha had a theory about Milo. It was simple. Because he was brought up by a welfare father, he lacked a strong paternal figure to model himself after. And, because he was a failed novelist, his father did not command Milo's respect. Milo needed dead modern artists to fill his void.

That night Milo dreamed his father was in a small room with a window looking out to a summery scene. His father was shirtless and hairy as he typed away on a manual Smith Corona. He was working on the same novel he always worked on, the one about his nympho first wife. He revised and revised, crumbling papers and throwing them to the floor. Next to his desk, the television played a black and white Robert Mitchum movie. The sound was off. A hot August breeze came through the window. His father was short, whiskered,

DEAD ARTIST

and wore his hair long. It fell into his dark green eyes. Milo and Samantha enter the room. Father Sonas says, "It's a pleasure to meet you Samantha, and you should be tickled to be with Milo." He stood. "I got wind through the grapevine that wonderful things are soon to transpire in his life, and he will soon be transported into the stratosphere of fame and immortality. I am very, very proud, like I always told him: don't do as I say, do as I do. No, that's not right. I mean, don't do as I do, do as I say. No, that's not right either." His father couldn't organize his thoughts. The words echoed, and then Milo woke up.

As Samantha slept beside him, she seemed to be smiling, as if she might have shared his dream. Milo thought about all that would be left when he was gone. The paintings, those captured moments, that is all that would remain, that is what he would be remembered for. His life would only be known for the way he made colors slide, or peel, or fold. It was all about the contrast of blue against yellow.

He mused. Maybe he would be remembered as the loneliest artist who ever lived, an artist who, by sheer luck, was rescued from desolation by Nick. He would be remembered as an artist with an estranged and angry brother named Ray who was so damn hard to get along with. Milo could never figure out his brother, so dark and handsome and yet so bitter. He was bestowed with luckier genes, yet could never be satisfied. Being a house painter could be frustrating for a would-be artist. After all his brother's only release came from his calculated seductions of the house wives mocked and imprisoned by the very white walls he painted. Ray had a keen ability to seduce other men's women. It always had to be another man's woman. He made love to these married ladies in their own homes, on the tarp. It was the risk of being discovered that made the fucking feel like it was shot up with crystal meth. And he was caught only twice, in one case the husband did not resort to gun or fist but instead he broke down, fell to his knees and wept. And then demanded to know the sexual details. As long as he knew each and every position, then he would not press charges. The other husband did fight Ray, with fists, and they duked it out John Wayne style, *mano o mano*, as top forty music played on the paint splattered transistor radio on the ground. The husband was beaten to a pulp, and this time it was the wife who broke down and wept.

Milo feared Ray.

And what was Milo to do with these scary thoughts concerning his own brother, where could he channel the thoughts that terrorized him? He didn't share them with anyone. Not even Samantha.

Anyway, Ray was through with the family, save neutral and good-natured brother Paul.

There were three brothers in the Sonas family. In the order of age they were, Paul, Ray, and the Milo.

Paul was kind and had callused hands from a life immersed in sand, sea, mountain and asphalt. Paul did it all. He scuba dived, surfed, rode a motorcycle, sailed, fished, skied, snow boarded, assembled Fourth of July rockets, mini boats. He even had a simulated rock climbing range in his own home. He was also the most consistently happy member of the family. His disposition was to agree with everything that was said to him, and avoid conflict.

"Paul is my half-brother but he is the only brother I have that is kind," Milo said to sleepy Samantha.

"What about your other brother Ray?"

"In one word, difficult, in four words, pain in the ass. He is estranged from the family and very bitter. I wish he would change. Recently he even alienated my sister Luna."

DEAD ARTIST

Luna and her family had been stranded at LAX, and called Ray to see if they could crash at his house until their morning flight and he turned them down cold. They spent the night in the airport. She vowed never to call him again.

This nuclear family had exploded.

But Nick was going to take Milo away from the cosmos of his family into another galaxy of celebrity and high society. But could Milo ever truly escape? After all, who were those faces that he repeatedly painted? Weren't they all subconscious portraits of his own family?

You are forever indebted to your parents. When your career sky rocketed in your youth it was your mother who stretched your canvases and it was your father who patiently, diligently and lovingly photographed them. You were their last hope. They were there for you at all the nightclub events and gallery shows. You have a debt that you cannot ever begin to repay.

Milo would always remember the nightclub called The Galaxy on Avenue B, it was there he had an event called "The Galaxy of Milo Sonas" and a sixteen millimeter documentary about Milo premiered that night. His father worked the projector high up in the balcony in that trendy run down club. When the cash first started pouring in, Milo supported his parents the best he could by paying them to do odd jobs for him, like putting together stereo systems, attaching Bose speakers to the loft bed, or painting fresh coats of white on some walls. He paid his mother to clean his studio and his father to photograph his paintings. He would take his parents out to breakfast, lunch, dinner. It was just the three of them. A gypsy network of three.

When Milo was young but getting older he sometimes felt guilty for becoming powerful and independent. He wanted to apologize to his parents for growing up, for becoming a man and for living on his own.

His father used to tell him to "Just do it!" long before this became a slogan for Nike.

Milo was roaming through Barnes and Noble. He saw the man with the gray hair at the cafe again. He was well groomed, with crew cut hair. He was clean shaven and his gait displayed impeccable posture. The man ordered the usual, a bagel and a mochachino.

How did these men become Barnes and Noble bachelors, living and feeding on whatever polite bits of kindness the employees provided, living on the hope that maybe today some woman browsing through current paperbacks might be the one?

Those who wander in the afternoon.

What about the other man Milo saw outside bus or taxi windows most afternoons? The man in the wheel chair who was legless and overweight, yet always took in the afternoon sun, be it the hot August sun or the cold February light. No matter the season this man was "out there" wheeling himself up the steep sidewalk like a sentry.

Or the Asian schizophrenic, dapper in his tight fitting secondhand suits who preferred the locally owned and smoke filled coffee shop that was peopled with scrappy post punk adolescents. That Asian man who was as silent as Buster Keaton and who busied himself through the day getting refills of coffee and filling his black pipe with tobacco and sucking on the smoke. Sometimes he would ask the barista for the phone book, and he would search for a business or a person. But he never made calls. He didn't have a phone.

DEAD ARTIST

These were the men who were always out when Milo was out, and so it got Milo thinking, was he also one of the lonely walking landmarks? Did people look at him and say, there goes so and so again? Men on the cusp of loitering. Maybe he was one of them after all? But Milo took solace in the hope that he had a way out.

"Enjoy your leisure time," Nick would say. "Because soon this business will take off and you are going to be very busy."

Milo mused as to whether there would come a day when he would miss his days of anonymity as he walked his dog past trees, and the people were shrouded and shaded within the beautiful green bubbles of their lives. He reminded himself that his impending success didn't mean that he was going to live forever, only that his paintings, like children and grandchildren, would survive him in white walled museum institutions where people from around the world would walk right up to them and if he was lucky, yawn.

Another regular in the army of afternoon wanderers was an aging anorexic lady who jogged in all white and wore oversized sunglasses like Jean Harlow. She was the last of the four lost souls that Milo repeatedly saw, and he wondered if he might become the fifth meandering musketeer, but for the grace of Nick's rescue mission. Milo feared he otherwise might become known as that forty something "artiste" who drank Earl Grey tea, chatted up unsuspecting college students and looked eternally boyish.

But Milo was to be saved, saved from becoming obsolete like vinyl recordings, typewriters and double feature drive-ins.

Samantha was napping knowing she had summer haystacks of time left in her life. She was his ticket to longevity. As Milo grew older his girlfriend became younger. Sometimes, when he painted, he felt like he was cheating time, in fact he felt like he was producing square babies made of color. And his children would live as long as acrylics lasted. And that was forecast to be a long time considering they were made of plastic.

When times became tough like this, and Milo felt defeated, Picasso would often brew some espresso, and tell him that he should, "always be painting."

Yes Milo should always be making more square babies.

Chapter Sixteen

Loneliness was not just a state of mind but a state of being, where one is unable to make connections anywhere in the constellation. It is a stagnant place where no e-mails could reach or where ringing phones cannot interrupt the silence.

Pablo materialized and asked Milo to explain to him exactly what it was like to feel so alone.

Milo's response: "The message that loneliness sends me is that I cannot penetrate otherness. It makes me feel stuck in sticky time. It is like some cold entity that refuses to comfort me. And it leaves me stranded in space....I begin to feel like an unsold canvas, or like fruit which has fallen off a tree that nobody picks up to eat, like a rotten apple rolling down a grassy hill in the heat, or like luggage unclaimed at the airport. The sight of others who look so happy with their tickets, standing in lines for movies, actually brings me pain. It is at times like this that I begin to relate to the Hunchback of Notre Dame. You know Pablo, I have to be careful or it might happen again."

"What might happen?"

"Well this feeling might snowball and maybe by this winter turn into an abominable snowman of self pity, and then boom, crack, boom I will be in the throes of another nervous breakdown."

"If you don't watch out, my friend, you are going to dig yourself into a hole. And bring it on yourself. Milo, you need to take a chill pill.

"Pablo, where did you learn that phrase?"

"I spend a lot of time listening and watching."

This was the calm before the storm. If Milo could just make it over this one last hump, well then he was almost *there* in the never-never world of what is commonly known as success.

Samantha woke after a long sleep. It was late in the evening, and she started to prepare pasta. "Milo?" She asked. "Do you think that we fell in love because of 9/11? Because before that it seemed as though we were drifting apart."

It was true. Prior to the attack on the Towers, they were severing their ties. But, after seeing the repeating images of the planes exploding into the towers, Milo phoned her and begged her to be with him. They both walked together through the vigils on Union Square. Crowds converged, there were spontaneous debates about country and causation, and acoustic guitar strumming *a la the sixties*, glowing candles on the sidewalks, and photographs of the missing began to appear tacked to walls and telephone booths. This must have been what it felt like to fall in love during the bombing in London during World War II. And oh, that night when Milo had to wrap a white tee shirt around his mouth to protect his lungs from the snowing ashes and mixed into that cocaine-like substance were the remains of the dead.

It was September 12 when something unforgettable happened to Milo and Samantha.

It rained very hard in New York City. The sound of thunder made them think of aerial bombings. Milo opened the door of his storefront to see the water cleansing the city, and to let in some much needed freshly washed air. And there in his doorway stood a rain drenched girl.

"You look very wet." Milo quipped, surprised by his statement of the obvious and his effort to sound witty.

DEAD ARTIST

"My umbrella broke. I just walked here from Ground Zero, I volunteered there all day."

So you offer this young stranger the use of your facilities, to dry off, you offer her a chance to take a warm shower and a change of clothing. The girl looks to be in her mid-twenties. She has that fresh yet budding maturity that twenty six year old women have. She is filled with frenetic energy. She tells you that she had been working at Ground Zero for twelve hours straight, she is covered with dust, the dust of the dead. She accepts the offer to shower. There are no walls to separate your bathroom from the rest of the studio and you find yourself watching as she peels off her wet denims and tank top. She steps naked into your closet-sized shower, and as you watch her, Samantha is watching you. "Just what are you planning here Milo?" Samantha says.

Samantha has an almost otherworldly understanding of you, a sort of shared brain. And though it might hurt her feelings she didn't deny the folly of your love making with its quick, jagged, jerky, laughter inducing antics, like an X-rated slapstick comedy. And you with your befuddled deadpan exuberance attempting to penetrate the impenetrable.

"Okay," Samantha says. "If this is what you want. I'm in."

"Thank you so much." Milo said, genuinely grateful. "Now listen if we are going to do this, we have to do this right." Now nervous, he added, "All of my past efforts at threesomes have failed. A collector of mine once advised me that the best way to get a threesome underway is to get 'nasty pronto.' So this is how we're going to proceed..." Milo moved from nervous to clinical.

He began taking off his clothing and he advised, well, ordered, Samantha to do the same, as quick as possible. Pronto.

"Oh my," Samantha said with a bemused smile. "Tell me you are not going to do what I think you are going to do."

"Tonight is a special night, Sam. The world is on fire. The city is smoldering. New York has been shattered. We are at war. It feels like the end of the world. If ever there was a time to get crazy, correction, nasty, it is now."

Naked, hairy, erect, giggling mischievously, Milo steps into the shower to discover the volunteer lathering herself luxuriously. She is tall, lithesome, clean and glistening. Milo's entrance is precise, aggressive, confident and is received soapily, favorably.

It is only later that Milo will feel remorse for hurting Samantha's feelings. After some slithering about with suds and skin, Milo signals with his wet arm for Samantha to join them, and she squeezes in. The three were sandwiched together in the stall shower as though in a nineteen seventies telephone booth during a thunderstorm. Confusion ensued when Samantha first entered the tiled shower stall and the three of them jockey for position, like passengers in an overcrowded rush hour subway car, pushing and maneuvering to gain territory.

Though Samantha tried, crouching on her knees proved to be dangerous to the stability of those standing, but it was sweet of her to attempt what she was attempting, which was to please both parties standing. Soon Samantha found herself crouching half in and half outside the shower as Milo and the Ground Zero volunteer eagerly made out like school kids. Once out of the shower, dripping, shimmering, the three of them traded kisses, naked in the narrow kitchen area. Each one in turn bumping their ass either into the mini fridge, the sink, or the laundry basket. Then they took it to the main area as Samantha and the 9/11 volunteer kissed on in a theatrical manner, as a show just for Milo's pleasure. Milo fiddled with the CD player, searching for Gato Barbieri's seductive jazz, and prayed that this time all would go well. Milo felt his erection subside as reality hit him hard. This might be the beginning of World War III. Armed US jets flew overhead, patrolling the no fly zone above New York City. Was this the time to throw morals to the wind when the reckoning, or the rapture might be soon at hand? Of course it was, he thought.

"I want to watch you two in action." The volunteer said slinking into a reclining mode. This request was the kiss of death to whatever sensual mood had so far been built. Entering Samantha was always a hit or miss proposition. Milo tried anyhow and this became a kind of exhibition. A clinical demonstration. A curiosity.

But feeling put under pressure to perform, Samantha, as expected clamped up, her leg nerves twitching and pulsating. Was Milo's threesome at risk?

"What's wrong?" The watcher asked.

"I have a condition, my muscles, they contract."

"Here let me relax you." The volunteer cooed. And next thing Milo knew the volunteer had her head buried between Samantha's knees, thereby putting to shame Milo's ability to relax a woman properly. Shame on his half-ass foreplay.

Milo thought back on that night now with mixed emotions and though the volunteer was sweet enough, he remembered how the next day she didn't awaken until 1:00pm. Then he had to ask her to leave because his mother surprised them with a visit to New York, and Milo strained to come up with an explanation as to why there was an extra naked woman sleeping in his loft bed. Milo didn't tell his mother the whole story, and after they woke the volunteer, she left with an awkward goodbye.

Samantha and Milo would always have 9/11, nobody could take that away from them.

The Thanksgiving after 9/11, Milo and Samantha broke up again.

The main reason for their falling out was Samantha's refusal to get out of bed and get in the taxi to go to the airport. The plan had been for her to come with him to Gold Haven and visit with his family.

When Milo returned disgruntled from his embarrassing family visit Samantha came to pick up some of the belongings that she had left behind and, as a kind farewell gesture to Milo, she purchased from him two works on paper and paid cash for them. They were the same works that he had promised to give to her for free before their post-9/11 breakup.

They were to get back together again years later when they were brought together by another New York event, the blackout of the northeastern United States. That night New Yorkers roamed the streets holding candles, and Milo wandered into Thompson Square Park holding the hand of an an attractive thirty year old stranger, and the two of them witnessed spontaneous bonfires in the park. Around the fire a circle of young folk sang, joked and threw debris to stoke the flames.

Milo and the pretty stranger had a pleasant enough time, but sure enough when her cell phone service resumed her interest waned and she made plans right in front of Milo to go see a friend.

Milo returned home defeated. Inside his studio it was hot and dark. He lit a match and found a candle. Just as he was preparing for sleep there was a knock at his storefront door.

"It's me," said an instantly recognizable female voice. It was Samantha.

Milo, still in his briefs opened the door and there she stood, dressed in her trademark frayed bell bottoms. She was with her friend who had wonderful dyed orange and pink hair, and a nasal septum piercing. The pair came in complete with a six pack of beer. Luckily Milo already had tequila in his pantry. Light had still not been restored, and all that was to take place that evening, took place in the faint flicker of candle light.

"We only seem to get together during disasters." Samantha said that night.

"Yes, I know, it's weird. You are like an angel that descends to watch over me during dark times."

"I'm your disaster girl."

Now the pilgrimage to Gold Haven to see Milo by bus, was the first first time they had reunited since the blackout. And it was the first time they were brought together by events other than terror, or the blackening of a city, or so Milo hoped.

Chapter Seventeen

Milo supposed there was no such thing as a good or convenient time for his mother to begin the painful, humbling and humiliating process of dying. But this was truly the worst possible time. His life was booming and blooming. She was in a final wilt.

Sunday, and cooling weather outside hints of what normally comes in September and October. Milo and Samantha walk Moon though a park where boys are playing touch football on a field. A perfect cool summer afternoon for Milo's favorite pastime, wandering.

Milo had to take some time off from the misery. After all, he is not the one who is dying. Sometimes it felt like his mother was pulling him like a rip tide, leading him away and out to sea, he had to keep reminding himself that he was not dying. Not yet.

Milo believed that each person has a North star they follow during lost times in their lives. And just as Vincent had Theo, Milo had his once headstrong, capable and omnipresent mother. Perhaps Samantha was becoming a newly prominent figure in his life, maybe a candidate for a replacement North star.

His mother blew his ego out of proportion from the very start. At age nine, she sat him down and told him two things: One, that if he wanted to be great in his life, that indeed he could do it. "If you want someday to be a great poet, or a great singer, or dancer, or artist, you can!" And two, "You have been touched by the gift." This rocketed his self esteem into the stratosphere, and from then on Milo felt himself to be beyond mere lowly school work, and the annoying black hole of history facts that teachers attempted to drill into him. Instead he lived in haphazard bliss and at the age of thirteen, both wrote his first novel and later that year modeled in clay a Rodin-esque bust of his grandfather. And so he spent his youth with buzzing, unstoppable confidence, and with foaming-to-the-brim arrogance. This creative underage intoxication kept him "high flying" for years. His whole life he felt like he was holding a flag, a flag that said, "watch me, hear me, caress me, read me."

And New Yorkers did, they really did...at least for a while.

Then during these past ten years when fame began to distance itself from him and then to completely sever their relationship, it left him standing alone, leaving him hanging until he came crashing to the ground of suburban anonymity. He blamed his mother for having falsely coerced him into believing that he was beyond education, structure, or the "yawn inducing" academic machine. And so he spent four years in hibernation, living in that government-sponsored room, near family, unsure of his future. But now that a powerful force of a man named Nick was putting his investment guns behind him, he could once again love his mother for all she had instilled in him. But it was too late now. She was fading.

His mother had been positively psychic in her ability to know and sense all that Milo was up to at all times. It was as if he was not his own person, ever. It was as if he belonged to her.

Milo stood forth proudly on each and every New York street, as customers snatched up his paintings, sometimes in minutes, he always knew he was onto something with his art. And his mother assured him through the years that, "some day, some how it will all come together for you."

The first fellow street artist that Milo stood next to on West Broadway was a man in his sixties who looked weathered and much older, his skin was like a wood carving in a cigar shop. And this man, in his equally wrinkled gray suit, upon hearing this was Milo's first day of selling on the street, had confided in him that years of street selling had brought him great happiness but it also had brought him to the abyss of two nervous breakdowns. The two of them often chatted on the street. He was once offered an exclusive contract in a gallery, the man rambled, "But I told em, nuthin fuckin doin unless you slap the gold and silver into my palm. That's right, I's got to see dat money honey, or nuthin doin. But you Milo, I promise you that one day, what that shit dat you do, dat real cool colorful shit, well mark my words, and mark them well because I can see the future baby and someday, somehow, somebody is going to come along and they are going to take you all the way there. Because what you got there, is what it takes." Then he turned and muttered to himself, "Mother fucker."

These were the only two times Milo had ever heard that phrase, "someday, somehow, some one..." Once from his mother, and the second time from the street worn man.

Milo's journey to this prophetic moment in time, was also soured by a nervous breakdown. He found himself in a week-by-week rental hotel. All he had was a simple white room, some posters from the Museum of Modern Art, his dog Moon that shaggy bohemian beast, and two artistic giants from the other world. And now he had Samantha too. But she was sleeping, always sleeping.

And though she is with you, you still feel so alone. Especially now at this bewitching hour of 3:00am, when the lonely must at least attempt to sleep. In this room with no damn air conditioning, no relief. Just a fan buzzing, blowing hot air around.

So you call him, the old night owl Dr. Hyatt. He takes calls twenty four hours a day.

But all he seems to say is the same repeating refrain, "I hope you do get rich, I really do."

You tell Dr. Hyatt that you have not heard from Nick in days. What is Nick doing? What's next? Nick had promised you, with a rather mysterious air, that he would be enlisting the help of certain VIPs to further your career.

Milo often wondered in the late night hours what would become of the thousands of paintings he made over these twenty years of paying his dues. Did they all still exist? Would all his hard work and dedication create a boomerang effect, and project good Karma back to him?

When the money finally came and Milo could fulfill his fantasies he planned to be a burly and bearded Rodin-like sculptor, working, molding monumental masses of clay that would be cast into bronze that would rust green in the elements of passing seasons. Huge muscle bound men, roughly rendered, bumpy, and women, young and gaunt, like heroin chic fawns, emerging from mounds of clay hillsides. Milo imagined that cranes would have to be employed to transport these giant bronze-toned odes to humanity. They would be landmarks, parked and poised in cities like Dallas, Toronto, St. Louis, Newark, Chicago. Bold bronzed, unschooled, untutored testaments to shape, contour, and silhouette.

"I'm not a painter," Milo said. "I will be a sculptor."

DEAD ARTIST

Pablo was smoking by the window, his hand no longer able to create in the after-life, "Tell me about it, I felt the same way."

Chapter Eighteen

"Over the past ten years, I have kept accounts of certain expenditures," his mother said, laying in her deathbed. "The breakfasts, the lunches, the small incidental petty cash loans. Those times that I rescued you when you couldn't pay your rent, your electric, your phone, the times when I bought you art supplies because you were broke, those times when I lent you twenty dollars to rescue your clothes from the cleaners. Well, I want you to know that I added it all up, and as you can imagine it is an astronomical figure."

"But things are happening now and the way it looks, I will be able to pay you back and then some."

"I just want you to know I have all these years visualized all that will happen for you. And even though I won't be alive to really see it, sometimes I can picture it in my dreams, I see you living on the French Riviera in a villa just like your second father Picasso. I can see it at night, in immense rooms with twenty foot ceilings and there you are working into the morning light. Just don't worry about thanking me for all that I have done for you all these years. Always remember you don't owe anybody anything. Life is not about paying people back."

Milo felt like he was knee deep in clay-like karmic debt. The big muddy.

There was Shelby, the Jewish accountant girl, he owed a lot to her. They had once been lovers in New York. She had run into him during a particularly dire summer dry spell, when he was so broke he could only afford to buy a knish for lunch. There he stood on Fifth

Avenue, she was walking by with her sister. Shelby took pity on him by buying one of his large paintings right there on the spot. Then she took him on like a pet project. She made sure his rent was paid, "so you can feel like a human being," is how she put it. She hired him to create an artsy poster for her accounting firm. She paid another month's rent, took him out to dinner, movies, and to the Gap and Old Navy to get jeans, shirts, sweaters, socks and briefs. Milo continued to make love to her as long as he could, that is, until he was out of his financial mess. And then Shelby gave Milo an ultimatum, she told him to give up his studio and to move into her Murray Hill apartment. "I will take care of everything for you," she said. She was petite but had a tremolo voice that carried. "All you have to do is give up one thing....other women. Or should I put it more succinctly, girls. Now I have a surprise for you, I bought us tickets to see Rent on Broadway, I bought three tickets, we can take your mother."

Milo seriously considered the proposition of being a kept man, protected from the rigors of street life by this lovely Jewish, high strung and extremely capable woman of thirty. He thought about her taut body, firm and flat chest. And then he took into consideration the appeal of the unknown. The unknown fortune to be made, the unmet women. And he knew very well that he had to be out in the streets, mingling on the edge and selling his art through the ever shifting temperaments of the art buying community and the changing seasons. He had to admit it, he was addicted to chance and there was a part of him that was also hooked on the extreme sport of loneliness. He wanted out of the sheltering relationship with Shelby and so one night he declined to make love to the sweet girl who was so good with numbers and she knew he was addicted to sex, and not the monogamous kind. She threw a dining room chair across her kitchen and watched him walk down the narrow railroad apartment halls of her fourth floor Murray Hill walk up and exit her front door.

Milo thought about Shelby and what might have been as he made a phone call to his brother from the hallway of his mother's house.

"Hey, it's Milo, how are you?"

"Pretty good, I just leased a new car. And they delivered it to my house forty five minutes after I made my down payment. It came as fast as a pizza delivery."

His brother Ray sounded unusually cheerful considering his mother was so close to death.

"That's good, glad you have a new car Ray... Well, it looks like the end of an era over here, so I am going to cut to the chase and ask you, are you going to fly out here or what?"

"Well, let me think about this for a moment. My wife and I are having a dinner party this week. We are having some dear friends over, and we are going to have an informal poetry reading afterward. I just don't see what the point of flying out there would do. Not sure if I am in the mood to bask in all that morbid negativity that I am sure is living, for now, in Mom's house."

"Nobody is basking in anything here. Mom is dying. So do you want to spend some time with her or not? She is still conscious and would very much like to see you."

"To be honest it sounds to me like a drag."

"Visiting your mother when she is dying is supposed to be a drag. I thought you knew that already. No, visiting your dying mother is not a trip to Disneyland, and it's not nearly as fun as your annual outings to Spain. But it is something that people do. Sons do it."

"But I am here doing interesting things with interesting people."

"Your mother is an interesting person and she happens to be dying. If I were you, I would find that pretty interesting."

"But..."

"But nothing. You didn't show for grandma's death or for Dad's. I thought maybe there might be a place in your heart to try to make it this time. But it seems very clear to me now, that you are a heartless fuck," Milo said, quite pleased with himself.

"Look, I don't want any more tragedy in my life. I have a life you know. A real life. My wife and I made a conscious decision years ago that we were going to do our own thing and that we weren't going to let the family be a distraction."

"And you have succeeded in turning your back on your family. What I am wondering here is if you can make a small concession in your routine to at least say goodbye to her. This is your only mother. You only get one."

"Okay, how 'bout this, I will think about it."

Milo's sister Luna was only two days into a vacation on the West Coast when she decided to cut her trip short and return to Gold Haven. Milo immediately embraced her and asked her about her trip. There was a flight cancellation and they were stuck in LA and Ray lived minutes away from the LAX so despite what happened last time, they called him and asked if they could stay in his new home overnight, till their 7am flight departure and again, he said no. And she told Milo frankly that she had had it with Ray. She said her youngest daughter cried profusely at the airport all night. Milo told her that Ray was trying to decide whether he would fly out to see their mother and Luna said, "You know something, I hope he doesn't come and I bet he won't. It would require him to have a heart and some human emotions and he doesn't have either."

They brought groceries from the supermarket and Luna served up a complex extravagant salad and iced coffee. It was a sticky hot summer day and it hardly seemed like appropriate dying weather. He remembered how Grandmother Sonas' life flickered out during the spring. But then again death has never been known to calibrate with appropriate seasons, and it didn't care about the weather.

Summer weather does not always mean summer cheer.

"Your brother is an ass," Vincent said. "There are no two ways about it." Vincent was sitting on the porch with the others, but they could not see him. He continued, "Your brother certainly doesn't compare to mine. Theo supported me financially my whole life, sending me all the art supplies that I needed, that's what made me feel the worst. It pained me to be such a burden to him."

Luna, her husband, and even their child seemed to just stop speaking and let the light and the heat surround them. Milo headed upstairs to his mother's room.

You gave up all your friendships. You fought with all your girlfriends. You lived on quarters and sacrificed an education just because you have this knack with color and line.

You have taken some big chances all right.

You have always had a love for old people. You were so close with your grandparents who were Mexican and who spoke English as broken as an old ox cart. Growing up in LA, your grandparents lived across the backyard swimming pool from you. And you often joined them for arroz con pollo. You used to watch bull fights with them in black and white on TV, and the Merv Griffin show, Lucille Ball, the Price is Right, the Dating Game. You have always been an old soul. Maybe that's why you like to spend your August afternoons in your mother's room.

With her head propped up against at least four pillows she says, "Milo, you have been mine all my life, my baby, but I am setting you free now. You haven't always known it, but I have been watching you all your life, like an angel. If Ray ever comes to see me, and I do doubt he will, don't let him think that the things he does affect you, don't let him bully you. Don't let him destroy you now. Not now that you are living on the cusp of your Picasso fantasy."

"Mother I hate to break it to you, but I don't think he is coming."

And then his mother frowned, that famous Sonas frown, which makes it feel like the angels were a no show.

Chapter Nineteen

That night Ray called. "I have done some thinking," he said to Milo, "and I am going to make the scene after all. Yes I am going to come out and visit Mom. I have a week vacation due me, I'll come out for the weekend. Don't worry about putting me up. I will stay in a hotel just to keep my sanity. I have already booked my flight. I arrive on July seventh." Ray said *arrive* as though his appearance equated with the second coming of Christ.

And with these words the dynamic of the family would change.

Already, Paul, the all around sportsman, was on his way, and so were cousin Adina with her husband and two kids. It seemed as though Mother Sonas was hanging onto life just long enough for everyone's flights to arrive safely.

"Mother, " Milo said sitting on her bed. "Everyone is flying out to see you. And yes, Ray is coming."

"Ray has decided to come?"

"Yes, Mom. Yes."

As his mother smiled, blood flowed to her cheeks flushing them with color like the last brush stroke of life's vitality. Once again his mother was experiencing a resurgence of strength, she was like a Phoenix rising. She suddenly longed to escape the confines of her bed, and she began to do the one thing that was her form of self expression, her release and her salvation; she began to vacuum the house. The suction sound of the vacuum, and the vibration on her hand brought her great joy. The parallel lines she forged on the old carpeting gave her satisfaction. But she soon tired, and then sat on her living room couch, just trying to steady her breath.

Meanwhile Milo never felt more vital, young and full of bubbling possibilities than when he was in the proximity of his dying mother. Her room's only light came from sunshine pressing yellow against the white curtains. There was a pitcher of water on the night table next to prescription medication jars which huddled like chess pieces. The TV was on with the volume down, two bronze tanned Latin lovers were quarreling in a Spanish novella on cable, and unread hardcover classics were sandwiched together on the bookshelves. They were thick books, which she, at this point would never have time to finish, books like *The Magic Mountain*, *Look Homeward Angel* and *Ulysses*. Consuelo, the Costa Rican nurse with her constant smile, timid, short, and stocky, dusted the books and swept the floor, and was always insisting that Mrs. Sonas halt her attempts to clean her own house. Sonia's bedroom was air-conditioned, cold as Christmas and the air was moist as a fern gully and musty as a used book store. It felt as though time had her cornered. Death has found this place. She could not hide. And after Milo broke the news that Ray was on the way, she seemed relieved. She thought about all of the perfectly healthy happy times he could have visited, yet he chose to come now, to pay homage to her... the tired half-self she had become.

"When he comes," she said to Milo, "I just hope that you two don't fight. I just don't have the strength to watch that."

"There is nothing left to fight about," Milo said.

"Don't go on and on about all the good things that are happening to you. I don't think that Ray will be able to take it, you have to remember that you are an artist and that he is a house painter who pines to be an artist. It is his life's lament."

"Okay, I will keep things to myself mother, don't worry."

Milo returned to his hotel room. Samantha left a note saying that she stepped out to have a smoke outside.

Milo lay back on his single bed. There was a part of him that wanted Samantha to go back to New York. He had become accustomed to his loneliness.

Loneliness was his friend and jealous mistress.

What does Loneliness say? "Shhh," it says. "Don't attempt to describe this indescribable feeling to anyone. This room, this city, this earth," Loneliness says, ".. is not for you."

Milo does something with his sorrow, with static time. He pours color onto a plate as if in a trance created by the urban rhythms of soul music on his radio. He props a canvas up on an aluminum table, and begins to paint. These shapes that he paints are beyond his personal issues. Beyond the tedium of his family dynamics. Pablo wants to paint too, but in the sixth, seventh or tenth dimension there is no such thing as painting.

There is no order, no rhyme or reason to the technique that Milo employs when he paints. Acrylics have no rules. When he works with water based acrylics, the whole experience is so very water logged. Milo drinks coffee and Perrier when he paints and has to piss often. He sets down his dark colors first and then haphazardly builds up a central image. Milo never washes out the color on his brush. He uses black to create definition and always pours out an ample amount of white paint. It is with white that he creates the illusion of light. Milo has no interest in background, he paints them out of focus, and they become defused "impressions" of possibilities. Is that someone else in the background? Is that some 19th century man with a top hat back there? Even Milo does not know. Now this plastic medium is beginning to harden and dry. The gel medium used to create shine and texture is emitting fumes. Coffee, diet coke, sparkling Perrier, perhaps a cigarette. All these stimulants are like God given energy. He urinates again and then returns to painting. All this activity is a perfect anecdote to the curse of unbearable longing and unquenchable desire and the pining for connection and that emptiness and that void Milo still feels even though Samantha has come to visit.

Soon Ray would come to this small city.

Soon Mother would be gone.

Soon Milo would shoot like a circus acrobat from a cannon, back into the metropolis of New York City. He just has to hang on.

On the Fourth of July, nurse Consuelo assures Milo that she can look after his mother while Milo and his nephew, Donny, head for the local fireworks without Samantha who preferred to stay at Milo's place and catch up on some sleep. Donny hops in the back seat, and he immediately rips into sarcasm, "Well Hello Milo Sonas the great artist, I'm so surprised to see you in public and where are your body guards?"

Milo shot back, in jestful banter "Well, I feel perfectly at home here in the South of France. No need for bodyguards."

"You know Milo," Donny says. "You should sit down and write a book or a movie about the way that you think your life is going to be. Now that would be funny!"

Milo and Donny walked through the small local park by the lake. The crowd was ninety-nine percent white. Young married couples were everywhere. And

Milo's half-black nephew sported a badly botched Mohawk.

"Man," Donny said, "I can't believe I am even out here with you when I could be smoking a spliff at home. This is total bullshit. I really can't take this scene when I am not high."

"You know Donny, you put me in an uncomfortable position by telling me that you are in possession of pot. I really should be reporting this to your mother."

"You do that and I will beat the hell out of you. I'm not shitting you. And you know that I am strong enough to do it."

Milo knew that his nephew was only kidding. But on the other hand this oversized teen was five foot nine, and two hundred and thirty pounds."

Milo remembered just a few years back, he was riding Donny's bike and he and a couple of his rambunctious twelve year old friends were in hot pursuit of Milo with their BB guns. A few blocks later five police squad cars surrounded Milo. Milo stood frozen on his undersized bike and raised his hands to surrender.

"I didn't steal this bike. It is my nephew's. I am just borrowing it."

One cop shouted, "You're not the perp. You are the victim. Aren't you?"

Milo was confused, "The victim of what?"

"You are being pursued by some black teenagers with a handgun."

"Oh, that's just my nephew Donny and his buddies. It's just a BB gun."

Half a block away two more cops were were surrounding Donny and his scrawny friends. They were told to throw down their guns and raise their hands. Milo's mother at this time was still in good health and she stepped outside and began to rant and rave to the cops and all that was missing was a soulful southern Tennessee Williams drawl, as she said, "Those boys come to bother my son in the afternoons. My son, he is not well, he is recovering from a nervous breakdown, and those boys, those boys who come in the afternoon, well they come to taunt my poor son. Those boys are nothing but trouble."

Yet Milo still enjoyed his time with Donny.

Milo spotted Pablo standing, cigarette in hand, by the lake, looking pensive and out of place. He was dressed in a white slightly oversized and loosely worn linen shirt, loosely fitting slacks, and sandals. Vincent stood next to him wearing a straw hat, looking deeply tanned, in Lee jeans, and T-shirt.

Milo felt personally responsible for them, as if it was somehow his fault that they were stuck here, loitering in time. Donny was unable to see the two artists. Milo gave Donny ten bucks and told him to purchase a candy apple or popcorn from the vending truck on the sidewalk. Milo had a few words with the two dead icons.

"This is the Fourth of July, very American, don't you love it?" Milo said to them.

Pablo answered, spitting into the lake, "I hate public gatherings. They make me queasy. I never bothered to go to embarrassing public displays of affection on my birthdays, in fact, I preferred to stay home and paint. I abhor mob mentality."

"I would like to paint the fireworks, but I didn't bring my easel and supplies," Vincent said.

"It's not fair," Pablo said to Vincent, "that you get to paint and I don't."

"I guess you just got stuck in the wrong dimension."

"Lucky in life, but unlucky in death," Pablo said.

"And the reverse is true for me, except for the loneliness that seems to follow me wherever I roam."

DEAD ARTIST

Milo spotted his high-strung half-sister Amelia further down the great lawn. She had been the first to arrive in Gold Haven and there she was in this festive park by Reeds Lake. She had just spent some quiet quality time in Mother's gloomy confines. She looked happy to throw a blanket down on the grass and had brought a thermos with coffee. She had not spotted Milo yet.

Vincent looked anxious, his red hair seemed to glow orange in the twilight, as he said, "We are here for you Milo. We have descended onto this place to christen those that have a chance. We are here to guide you so you don't go down the wrong crooked path. We won't be here for long. Soon you will be on your own. Go be with your sister. You spend altogether too much time with us as it is."

"Okay, you're right. I will see you both later. Try to have some fun, would you?"

Milo sat down on the big blanket next to his half-sister who now, three times divorced was pushing sixty and openly admitting to having given up on love permanently. They sat in silence for awhile before Milo shared with her his fears for the future. He was wondering if Samantha was right for him, he found her to be a lazy girl. She was presently back at his hotel sleeping, This comment from him triggered in Amelia the desire to loudly lecture him on the ways of love. Amelia had a piccolo voice which pierced through sound barriers like an arrow of shrill sound. And she was telling him to stop this relentless hunt for beautiful women, including Samantha.

"Don't you see Milo that Samantha is just a little squirt. I mean, what kind of a person naps through the Fourth of July but a lazy little girl."

Milo pointed out that Bruce Willis who was well into his fifties notoriously dated a twenty five year old chanteuse of cinema. Nicholas Cage married a nineteen year old hostess from an LA sushi bar. And Picasso, well, we all know Picasso loved young babes.

Amelia said, "But you are not Bruce Willis, Nicholas Cage, or Picasso."

Milo felt deflated. "But when Nick gets things going, I will be a household name. That is if he can really pull this off. I hope he can. Amelia? Do you think it is really going to happen for me?"

"Milo, ever since I got here I have noticed that you have been filled with anxiety and fear. You can't let yourself be that way. You have to understand that things happen for a reason. There is a reason it is all happening now. Maybe before, you weren't ready for it all." The way that she pronounced *anxiety and fear* made her voice carry in the breeze past the picnicking families and it seemed to Milo like those words whisked and crackled like fireworks. It felt like she had written those words in flashing red, white and blue sparkles in the 4th of July night sky.

"Boy, your half-sister can be a real bitch," Vincent said. Milo didn't notice that they were now both sitting in the grass behind him. Vincent knew that Amelia could not hear him. She was not sufficiently sensitive to be privy to the voices of dead artists.

"You shouldn't let her talk to you that way," Pablo said. "At least answer her back. You are a man, be a man."

"Look Amelia." Milo said, standing up for himself, "Of course I am filled with fear and anxiety, my whole life now hangs in the balance, how much time is there really left for me. Maybe half a lifetime, and not necessarily the good half."

"You are totally obsessed with celebrity. Did you know that?"

DEAD ARTIST

The sky had grown sufficiently dark and the fireworks were beginning. Paint splatters of light in deep blues lit up the sky.

"Look I have no other choice but to become famous. I have nothing to fall back on. No other skills. I am so geographically challenged that I am not even sure where on this planet I live. All that I know about are shapes and faces. Life has me cornered. I am at the end of the line. I live in a fucking hotel that rents by the month. I get high just walking down the hall from all the pot smoked in the building, and that tangy smell of crack cocaine seeps through the walls. The people that roam the halls remind me of the denizens in *Night of the Living Dead*. Before Nick called me, I was a nobody, nothing. I was tired. I was exhausted from twenty years of hustling my art next to vendors that sold candied peanuts, hot dogs, gyros and freaking falafels."

Milo's spontaneous monologue of defeatism competed with the spark and crackle and boom of the fireworks. "But all this time, I never stopped believing, even as my canvases were blown down the street by gusts of wind. I knew that I had talent and that I knew how to make something that people wanted. And now Amelia, I have been given this chance to be something, to be someone... and you know something, I am going to take it. But at the same time I think about things a lot. For instance I feel badly that Mom won't be able to see and share in all that is about to transpire."

"You are just going to have to let that go. She is my mother too, you know, we both have to learn how to let...to let her go."

On this Independence Day, was there some place inside Milo where he looked forward to his mother's death? Would that day be the one when he was set free? When he was finally emancipated?

When his career crashed and he returned to Michigan everything for the first few years felt like a second childhood. Like the time spent with his nephew as an unlikely and unruly sidekick. The two of them up to no good in the afternoon. It seemed so long ago, just yesterday it seemed Donny was a boy, and it seemed like Milo had a boyhood too, once again.

Chapter Twenty

Dead artists did not come like archangels to visit his brother as he meticulously primed the walls of another home like a madman priming the walls of his asylum.

He was pressing some wealthy man's wife up against the plasterboard as she revealed to him that her husband hardly touched her and that she would surely soon be leaving him, but it was not the practical thing to do at this time. Now she backed him up against the wall, which kicked up a little white cocaine-like plaster dust. He already felt cornered by fate, which had rendered him talentless. He too tried his hand at painting, but due to a lack of draftsmanship ability, he was doomed to a world of abstraction. Not out of choice, because if he had a choice he would make the paintings that he saw in his dreams. He wished he could paint sci-fi fantasies where Herculean men floated in cosmos with their voluptuous female counterparts, scantily-clad like Greek slaves. As he kissed this other woman, Ray thought of his wife and her fashionable but prematurely white hair and how it seemed to him that she too was having an affair, not with a man but with her indulgent need to compete in poetry slams with performers half her age. As he lay this other man's wife down on the tarp of the interior of her unfurnished home, and began the monotony of undressing her, Ray found himself preoccupied by a plan. His flight to Gold Haven was already booked for 6:45 that evening. The plan was simple, and it was to destroy his brother's chance at new found success.

Before, it had been Milo who was obsessed with his sister Becky's success as a director of TV ads. In fact Milo had let the thought of his sister's financial success snowball inside him. It had become so extreme, that whenever he closed his eyes, he would see her smiling tightly from a recent face lift. Milo never understood until then how simple reoccurring thoughts can grow into disturbing concepts so big that they enter the mind like the foot of Goya's giant, destroying everything else, including the rational thoughts that come into their path.

During a particular drought in his finances Becky had sent him a check for fifteen grand and that loving gift had siphoned off all the manhood within him. When Milo deposited the check, he studied the word "gift" written on it, and it dawned on him he that would never make any real money in his lifetime. And he remembered how she had once said to him, "If I had to live in that tiny studio of yours I would have killed myself a long time ago." He had heard that refrain before.

Again Milo's thoughts were filled with suspicion that reality was orchestrated in such a way that after he created a magnificent body of work and shipped it to New York, he would die in some inexplicable manner and then a gallery exhibit would be held posthumously and yield enormous wealth. The only question was, who wanted him dead?

Becky had been getting a reputation for being difficult due to her burning ambition to direct a major motion picture. She had turned down many commercial accounts to keep her schedule clear for such a project. How did she feel about Milo's new opportunity? And of course there was Ray who was surrounded by the white interiors that he painted, driving himself mad. And Luna who had been a child celebrity, certainly she wasn't thrilled with the possibility that her youngest brother might eclipse her. Which of these souls wanted Milo dead? Who would have the guts? Who had the motivation?

As Milo walked through life he kept these *fears and anxieties,* as Amelia called them, neatly checked at the door. Milo tried to carry on despite the fact that he always perceived his life to be in mortal danger.

Chapter Twenty-One

"She is coming, her name is Carly," Samantha said to Vincent with her kind smile. "And she is a very pretty girl, very pretty, I hope you like red heads. I immediately thought she would be the most perfect of all my girlfriends because she had so many of your prints on her dorm walls. The few times we got high together she had told me that she often believed that she was born in the wrong century. Carly always said she wanted to be a Dutch girl in the early part of the 19th century." Samantha expertly rolled herself a cigarette on the fire escape outside Milo's room.

Milo wondered aloud, "How did you ever convince a girlfriend of yours to travel across the country from New York City to boring Michigan to meet Vincent."

"Well, I'll just put it to you this way, I told her that I met this boy, I refer to all men as boys, and I said he was a painter, a loner. I told her he had an angular face and a tortured soul. And I told her his name just happened to be Vincent. And she, who I believe was high when I called her, took this as some sort of divine intervention or something and she was sure that this meant that he was the one for her."

"So is she coming by bus or plane?"

"Neither...she is hitchhiking here."

"Isn't that awfully dangerous for a college girl?"

"She is twenty five, and she is extremely street smart. I am not worried about her in the least."

"When will she get here?"

"In a couple of days."

It was decided that in preparation for this love match that Vincent Van Gogh be properly groomed and that he should most definitely purchase some new clothing, preferably from the Gap, Old Navy, or Steve and Barry's.

Milo and Samantha took Vincent to Supercuts, where his wild mane of hair was cut, styled, and blow-dried. Fortunately Vincent had insisted that he didn't want a short cut. So instead he was given just a slightly shorter but more layered version of messy, and they were assured by the sensual stylist who had a dash of bright blue in her jet black hair, that this was an up-to-the-minute look for a guy. So much wonderment had entered Milo's life via Samantha on this overcast July day. He wished his mother could share in all that was bursting forth in color bright and yellow as the sunflowers that Vincent had painted.

One afternoon as Samantha was taking her astonishingly long, sumptuous summer afternoon nap accompanied by Milo's equally sleepy dog, Milo decided to take the bus to visit his mother in her gloom.

Milo entered into his mother's dreadfully stale room with every intention of talking her out of her own death. He had convinced himself that she had chosen to die under the mistaken belief that she was no longer needed. She was taking his success as a cue to bow out of life. Milo had always been the most needy member of the Sonas family.

"Mother," he said, squeezing next to her on her bed. They both now lay side by side. He tried to imagine what it might be like to be at the end of life's journey.

His mother was breathing through tubes, and the machine was sighing in and sighing out. It was hypnotic in its new age repetition. Milo found himself breathing in sync with the apparatus.

"Are you sure that this is really what you want to be doing?" Milo whispered to her. "Is this really the right time to die? Now that I am on the brink of so many great accomplishments I want you to be there when I marry, when I have my first child. Isn't that worth sticking around for?"

"So you are getting married," she said as if she were talking in her sleep.

"There is a girl that has come back into my life."

"This is the first I hear of it." It wasn't.

"She just kind of just showed up out of the blue, at my doorstep so to speak. Remember Samantha? Remember the girl that was with me in New York during 9/11? Well, guess what, she missed me, and she caught a Greyhound bus out here to see me." Milo sought recognition in his mother's face.

Sonia Sonas found some strength. "She took a bus all the way from New York? How exhausting, she could have gotten a plane ticket online for practically the same price. She must be totally worn out from the trip. I once took a bus trip and it nearly killed me. There was a man sitting next to me who told me that he had just been released from prison. He even went as far as to show me that he was packing a knife. He told me that he never went anywhere without his hunting knife. What a fright! I guess it all goes to prove that if she is willing to sit in a God-awful bus from the east coast to Michigan, all to see you; then it must really be love and I would seriously suggest you go for this opportunity while it is here."

"That's kinda what I came here to tell you, I am seriously considering it. Here I am with half my life over and believe me, I want to move on to the next level right away. Mom, I want you to be alive to see it."

"That isn't likely unless you get married within the next forty eight hours. I am slipping away quickly here, and I am not even sure how much longer I even want to hold on to life. It doesn't seem worth it. My quality of life is not ideal, you should see my body, it is pock marked with bed sores. I really don't see myself as having any more of these spontaneous recoveries. I never thought I would live to say this but Milo, but I want to die."

"Please don't."

"But it is how I feel."

"I don't believe you."

"I am being totally honest. I want out."

Milo, with his eyes welling up told his mother that he would like to make immediate arrangements for a wedding while she is still alive to see it.

Her answer came after a pause in which she found it hard to regain her breath, but finally she said softly, "Be careful. If you don't move quickly you are going to have a funeral and a wedding both on the same day. Ha! You know what they say, the three biggest events in a man's life is birth, marriage, and death. All we would need is somebody to pop a baby out on that day and the totality of the day would be complete."

The more Milo thought about it, the more he was sure that this was what he wanted to do. What better time than now, all his brothers and sisters were flying out to Gold Haven to be with their mother at her deathbed -- what a perfect time for a dual event.

Would his mother agree to such an innovation? And how about Samantha...would she go for it?

Chapter Twenty-Two

Samantha:
Milo asked me to marry him this evening.

Well, I didn't come out to the Midwest to see him with any expectations. No. I came out here because Milo will always hold a special place in my heart, being that we were together during that one moment when it felt like New York City was one big, broken, but happy family.

But I like his idea. In fact I love it. Yes, I am willing to marry him even though I know in my heart that he is doing it all for show for his mother. But I know how important it is for him to feel more complete and to show his mother that he has achieved something like completeness.

I want to do this for him.

I have always felt more comfortable giving.

Chapter Twenty-Three

Milo's half-sister Amelia was taken aback by the concept of Milo's hasty nuptials. A cigarette dangled from her lips as she watered their mother's lawn. She told Milo that he was once again trying to steal the lion's share of attention in the family. And, the idea of a pre-funeral tribute to his mother was downright morbid.

Ray got wind of the concept in Chicago's O'Hare airport en route to Gold Haven. Amelia had called him on his cell. This was the match to his gushing fuel. It truly motivated him to get his ass on that connecting flight and get to Gold Haven as fast as technology would jet him there so that he could destroy everything and everyone in his path, and have a good vacation at the same time.

Ray:

I look out over the clouds I see on this short connecting flight from Chicago to Gold Haven, and all I can think about is the blinding white that I use to cover the interiors of homes. Opaque white, solid white, off white, egg shell white, whatever. And, I wonder, as I look out over these pornographic pillows, bosoms, thighs, and cupid-like butt cheeks of clouds, what the fuck do I know about painting?

Most of the time I just draw a blank in front of those floor-stretched tarp canvases. Milo, that prolific dweeb, never runs out of ideas. I knock knock and knock at the closed door of my imagination, but nobody's home. Nobody answers. Each night I read voraciously to fill my mind with color, yet nothing seems to register. Nothing sticks. Sure, I can bullshit my way through the meaningless repartee at gallery opening cocktail events. I sound like a real artist. I stand there, aloof, unshaven, like Milo, unsmiling. But deep down I'm nothing.

Okay, so I haven't found my way in the world. Is that such a fucking crime, to be still searching as I push fifty?

It wasn't such a crime as long as everyone else floundered. Becky, with her pipe dreams of directing a feature film. Amelia, with another failed marriage, and Luna's crazy bastard adopted son Donny stealing cash from her safe just to buy drugs that will keep him out of professional sports. He'll never be that future millionaire. None of them are going anywhere.

Fuck! But Milo got a break. I felt okay about my monotonous life, applying layers of white over other layers of white and my dabbles at abstract art. I felt okay about my colorful improvisations on canvas, which might look pretty good if I knew when to stop and leave well enough alone before they become muddy and turn gray and brown like dirt after some rainfall. Yeah, I felt pretty good as long as my little brother Milo was living in a flea bag hotel in Gold Haven. The bastard was one step away from being homeless. But now, aside from being discovered again, he goes and decides to throw an impromptu wedding just in the nick of time before my Mom kicks the bucket. Frankly, this is just too much for me to take. And as God is my witness, there must a way for me to well... fuck it up.

Chapter Twenty-Four

Van Gogh, as expected, was extremely nervous
about the prospect of a real live New York City
university beauty traveling hundreds of miles just to
meet him. He drank a lot. His preference was Total
Vodka, which Milo had stowed away cases of since the
early nineties, when he, along with some famous Pop
artists had done an ad for their international campaign.
And that very ad just happened to be a pop styled
depiction of Van Gogh posing next to a Total bottle.
Now, things were certainly coming full circle as
Vincent gulped down the Total Citron mixed with
orange juice, ice and a sliced lemon topper.

Milo's mind ventured back to the day when he got
the deal with Total. He had only six dollars that day,
and he knew that the CEO would be coming to a club
event Milo was throwing that night. He ventured out to
the Utrecht Art store on Fifth Avenue and 12th Street
and asked the store manager to give him whatever
scrap poster board they were planning to discard. The
young bearded grungy looking manager was kind to
young artists and often cut them a break on prices. Milo
gave the manager three bucks in good faith. And he, in
turn gave Milo some damaged poster paper in colors of
white, blue and magenta. He also gave Milo some
white and red paint and two jumbo sized Pilot markers.

That afternoon Milo created the Total painting in a
mad rush. He had a hot date with a blonde Columbia
University coed that night and with his remaining three
dollars he purchased the cheapest bottle of Chilean

wine that he could find. The wine cost two dollars. He had one buck left to his name, Milo Sonas.

At 9:00 pm the blonde arrived, looking her age, eighteen; complete with upper braces, curly blonde hair, and wearing a tight fitting black evening gown. He offered her wine as he put the last touches of black outline definition on two Total Vodka paintings. Milo didn't have enough money to even take a subway with his date to the nightclub event, but as before he functioned on luck and synchronicity. A wealthy patron called him from Toronto and when he heard that Milo was dead broke on this night of rare opportunity, close in on a deal with Total and that Milo had a date and was down to his last dollar, the Toronto patron called up for a town car to whisk Milo, his freshly painted artwork and the pretty blonde college student to the event.

With electric black tape Milo attached the two finished paintings to the walls of the club and when the VIPs in suits arrived and witnessed the colorful, radical depiction of Vincent Van Gogh juxtaposed with the Total bottle, the dapper English CEO of Total importers said to Milo, "Anybody that can do that in one afternoon deserves the whole deal."

Now, twenty years later, who would have dreamed that Milo would end up in a hole in the wall hotel room, paying twenty five bucks a month, and getting afterlife visitations from the wanderlust spirit of Van Gogh who was now caught between the living and the dead? And who would have thought that Milo would now be instrumental in possibly providing Vincent's spirit with what was probably its last hope of finding love?

Milo hadn't heard from Pablo for a couple of days. Perhaps he was off womanizing and continuing his streak of being wildly successful with the ladies many of whom were miraculously able to see him quite clearly and feel his body as well. Unfortunately for Pablo he had no nerve endings, and felt nothing in return.

Picasso was experiencing great artistic frustration. He was unable to produce art and to channel his formidable energies. Van Gogh could create a painting, but it would disappear as soon as it was finished. Perhaps this was the universe's protection against becoming too dense with man-made objects. And so these two dead artists hung around Milo in the hope of channeling through him. And both, Pablo and Vincent, admired Milo despite the fact that he worked in acrylics, instead of the fragrant richness of the oils that they were most accustomed to.

"When did they first come into your life?" Samantha asked Milo as they drank sugary lattes at the local Barnes & Noble bookstore. The mostly conservative locals did not fathom the age difference between Samantha and Milo, since his boyish features never betrayed his true age; and his jovial smile, that is when he did smile, had a blinding effect on the local ladies. Milo, like an aspiring actor, never disclosed his age, even to Samantha. She was positive that Milo hovered forever somewhere just over thirty five.

"Let's see, when did they come into my life? They came to me one afternoon while I was painting. They never told me what or how to paint, never coaxed me, prodded me, or asked me to change my style. They just *Poof!* appeared, rolled cigarettes, drank my coffee and watched with envy. It was really just recently, right after Nick sent me more art supplies than I have ever had in my life."

"You are so lucky it is happening to you at such an early age."

Samantha may have been flattering Milo with that remark about his "early age." But Milo knew the truth, it was happening in the middle of his life, and just a little too late for his liking.

Before Samantha arrived, before the dead artists appeared and before Nick christened Milo with hope; Milo, in his hotel studio had felt frozen in time. All winter long, static cold energy seemed to surround him, chill him. He was wrapped in the uncaring arms of loneliness, and wandered the streets and wallowed in unquenchable self pity. During long late night dialogues with Dr. Hyatt, he tried to understand exactly why it was so impossible for him to puncture the frozen bubble that surrounded him, and why that bubble always made him feel so utterly alone.

For the first time Milo noticed on Samantha signs of bruising around the eyes. Samantha felt his gaze and responded, "I was wondering when you were going to notice that, considering you are a visual artist it sure took you a long time."

Samantha explained that she had a boyfriend over the past few years. She said she didn't like the person she had become when she was with him. She didn't like the arguing, the fights, the verbal and physical abuse. He brought out the worst side of her. She said that the two of them had a kind of "accidental" fall. "It was more my fault than his," she said. "At least that's what the judge said. The judge also advised us to keep a distance from each other."

It seems that her boyfriend was carrying laundry down the steps of their apartment building and she, like an angered bull, charged him and they both tumbled down the steps.

"I have never seen that angry side of you," Milo said. "What is it that the two of you fought about?"

"We fought about the same thing that every guy fights with me about. You know, my condition, my...tight pussy. Sometimes I feel like a character in a porno fable on DVD where all the men in some enchanted kingdom attempt to get inside the body of the princess in her castle, but I, the thigh-clenching princess will not allow anybody to enter. My pussy is my chastity belt. Until one day one gallant young man is able to penetrate my fortress."

"I'm not so sure if I'm the man for that job," Milo joked, to ease the tension. "It is a tough job, and requires a gallantry and precision that I, quite frankly, don't possess."

"Well, join the club. What can I say except that men get pissed off if they are denied entry into their significant other. And you know what, it makes me feel like I have become a virgin all over again. Hey, maybe I have been saving myself for you."

"But I can't get in there either."

"You will Milo, when the time is right."

The next afternoon Milo sat down for coffee at a newly built Starbucks and had a talk with Pablo about the unusually awkward erotic predicament he was in with Samantha.

Pablo retorted with, "I would not stay with a woman like that. A man must consummate with his woman, otherwise he is supplicating to the woman. A man should not have to beg."

"Sure, it's frustrating, but I am still happy that she made it out here during this difficult time."

Outside it was another lovely day in July, the clouds looked as white as freshly primed canvases and the baby blue color of the sky reminded Milo that light blue might possibly be his favorite color. He used the color obsessively. As a boy he once believed that if he used this color as much as possible that maybe his eyes might turn blue, or better yet that one day it might be acceptable for a man to wear blue lipstick, and blue eyeliner, or maybe dye his hair blue.

"Perhaps you see her as a challenge," Pablo said, cigarette butt dangling from his mouth, and his eyes squinting from the puffs of smoke like a gunslinger in a spaghetti western. "The only good thing about a challenge is triumph. As you know, I never try, I succeed. But no matter what I say, you will do as you wish."

Milo explained that Samantha reminded him of a time that he strangely found to be most romantic, the days following 9/11, that post-apocalyptic time in New York City, a time when Samantha and he used to roam the downtown streets. Her university was a couple of blocks from Ground Zero. That morning, she overslept and had to catch a later subway. Otherwise, she would have been at the train station at One World Trade Center when the buildings came down. This bit of lucky fate boosted her out of a minor depression and strangely raised her self- esteem level. Perhaps there was a reason for her life after all. Why else would she be spared? Milo and she both felt that somehow the attacks made them feel proud to be living in a city that was the center of world attention.

"That's just craziness," Pablo said. "I wouldn't pay that girl any mind. And I think you should have painted on 9/11. I painted constantly through the war. You know Milo I truly hope that this new art dealer really does it for you. I don't want to see you wind up like those other characters you see in the book stores and the coffee shops just wandering the afternoons and evenings away. I used to see those types in the cafes in Paris. Except for the crazy ones, most were there for the same reason, endlessly killing time waiting for success."

The barista then interrupted their conversation to ask Milo a question. The young man explained that he had been asked to paint a logo for the coffee shop and he wanted to know how he should go about charging for his work. The young man was unable to see Picasso.

Milo gave him some advice. "Okay, here's what always worked for me. Young artists tend to price themselves either too high, or too low. Too low and you are underselling yourself, too high and you lose the commission. So what you must do is ask the owner of the restaurant what his budget is for the art. This will put him in the hot seat, and chances are that he will quote a higher price than you expect. I once was going to do a mural for a fashion boutique showroom, I was broke at the time, and in my desperation I was prepared to do the job for a mere eight hundred bucks. But then I held my tongue, paused, and used silence as a tool, sometimes silence can be the best negotiator, and I asked them how much they had in their budget for the artwork and to my happy surprise they told me that it was ten grand. So I got smart and asked them for ten thousand and five hundred. Always add just a little bit more, so that they don't feel tempted to bring it down a notch."

The young man shook Milo's hand and thanked him for the advice.

Pablo said, "That was very good advice. But my advice would have been to tell the owner of the restaurant that I would be happy to do the job in exchange for one year of free dinners. For a young artist this sort of arrangement is best, guaranteed food and no starvation."

"I don't think the owner of any place out here would go for that."

"Then damn them. Nobody who is trying to become a truly great artist should be painting signs. There is no prestige in that."

"Come on, the kid is just getting started. He needs to test his wings."

Now Pablo added, "And besides that, you should have told him that no artist worth his salt should be living in Gold Haven, Michigan. He should be getting on the next flight out of this tiny city and immediately take up residence in London, Paris, Rome, New York, Barcelona or Berlin. This is no place for an artist. It is far too provincial. By the way, when the hell are you going to export yourself out of here?"

"Nick will be making arrangements for that very soon."

"What is stopping him from taking care of that immediately? You are treading water here in this wasteland by the Great Lakes. It is imperative that you be delivered from this mundane suburbia."

"Nick is currently taking care of some health issues."

"What health issues?" Pablo asked. "Who gives a damn about health?" In death as in life Pablo was oblivious to these matters, having been a chain smoker and living well into his nineties. He continued smoking, well into his afterlife too.

That Barnes & Noble was as close to a Parisian cafe as they could get to in that sleepy town of Gold Haven and Milo explained to Pablo that Nick was a man of 50 who was presently undergoing a hair transplant.

"Hair transplant? Who cares about hair? I lost most of mine and I was still a force to be reckoned with."

Milo went on to explain that it was imperative to Milo's artistic future that this entrepreneur maintain his self-esteem. Milo was keenly aware that this was his last chance at fame and fortune. He had hustled and scratched, and clawed his way about as far as he could take it. Disappearing from the New York scene was possibly the best thing that had ever happened to his career. The only better way that he could have furthered his career would be if he would have died.

Milo Sonas. Dead artist.

Milo Sonas, with his consistent relentless appearances in the streets of Soho, 5th Avenue, 6th Avenue and Union Square, as well as countless other spots made him about as famous as any building there; and now Milo Sonas, human landmark, was gone, much like the World Trade Center Towers. Oh what a terrible yet wonderful gift that clinical depression had given him. There was one song in the world that perfectly captured Milo's sense of metropolitan longing. It was Luther Vandross' rendition of *A House is not a Home*.

When I climb the stairs, and turn the keys, please be there, and still in love with me.

It was in this song that Luther's crooning, swooping voice captured what it was like to have love always just out of reach and what it would feel like to lose love. Milo thought back to what it was that caused his breakup with Samantha on that Thanksgiving just after 9/11. Milo and Samantha were scheduled to fly out to Gold Haven together to visit with his family on a 7:00 am flight.

"Why didn't you get on that flight and come with me to Gold Haven?" Milo asked Samantha as she sat on his fire escape.

"I can't stand getting up that early in the morning. To be honest, I felt pressured. I hate meeting a guy's parents under any circumstances. Parents usually end up hating me. So maybe it was a good thing. You know what they say, everything happens for a reason."

"I don't believe in that." Milo was obstinate about spiritual clichés. "But today," he said, "I will give it the benefit of the doubt."

He was taking refuge in her words. She was soothing him, lulling him into a feeling of safety. With her, his loneliness, like a shy phantom, had disappeared. He was so accustomed to wallowing in self pity that when it subsided, he didn't know what to place in its void. Loneliness had become his constant companion.

Samantha had a thing about sleep. She loved to sleep in and to nap, and it was that horizontal sleepy nature that had left him high and dry on that oh so imperative Thanksgiving after 9/11. Yet it was also her sleepy nature that endeared her to him. He decided to let go of his resentment. He forgave her.

All of his paintings were now gone, they had been trucked to the East Coast, and they were now being scanned in order that they be turned into Giclée prints. Nick had promised to take Milo's career all the way to the Guggenheim.

Milo thought back to the moment when the trucks came with stacks of white canvases for him to paint on. And he had to send the first batch back because the wood frames were too thin, they were not the heavy duty size that Milo preferred. And then the boxes and boxes of paint came next, gallons of white, black, gloss medium, and then 32 ounce jars of color, more than he had ever seen outside of an art supply store. It was thousands of dollars worth of paint. More paint than he had ever had at one time in his whole life.

He remembered when he and Nick had gone to Pearl Paint on Canal Street in New York. Four sales reps helped them as Milo pulled every color and brush off the shelf and put them into baskets. Then downstairs, in the basement of the largest paint store in the world, they pulled dozens of pre-stretched canvases, and were still grabbing more and more supplies as the sales clerks tried to catch up with them. Nick, Milo and the sales reps were at it until the store closed. But then it occurred to Nick that it might be cheaper to order online, so he told the reps to put the merchandise on a twenty-four hour hold. Then, Nick ended up ordering on the internet.

"But will you be getting anything at all from yesterday's order?" the Pearl Paint manager asked, his voice cracking on the phone.

"I'm afraid not," Nick said, canceling the order. The store manager's heart was broken.

Nick was a scrupulous businessman. Nick had the money. Nick had the power. Nick was transforming Milo's life.

"The word is," Nick said, "that you had what it took to make it all along. But the galleries would not touch your work because you were out on the streets undercutting their prices. It was your total disappearance from the scene, that created the possibility of your becoming now what you should have been all along, a superstar in the art world and a household name."

With all this going on, Milo still felt old. He felt time running out. He wanted to change his identity and transform himself into a Papa figure. He wished he could just let himself get thick and fat. He wanted to name his first daughter Matisse and first his boy Miro, the second girl would be named Georgia, after a beautiful and mentally ill character in his favorite Italian six hour epic movie called, *The Best of Youth* which told the story of the handsomely tortured soul of Mateo and his sensible and strong brother Nicoli. Milo wished his own brother Ray was less of a Mateo and more like Nicoli.

Unbeknownst to Milo his brother was on his way to change the course of Milo's trajectory.

Why does there always have to be a spoiler? A bad apple?

Ray had always been, or so it seemed, an angry child. From as early as Milo could remember he envied Milo's constant creative flow. And he discouraged Milo at every turn.

At nine Milo was obsessed with the drawings of Michelangelo, and sketched from them to the point of obsession. Ray told Milo that Michelangelo was gay, and that the drawings were of men fucking and that Milo was a faggot for loving Michelangelo.

And when some maniac took a sledge hammer to the Pieta, Ray taunted Milo saying, "The Madonna's head is next, and then he's going to come after you."

Ray had kept Milo on edge, often holding their male dog in his arms when it had an erection and chasing Milo around the house attempting to thrust the dogs red penis into Milo's face.

And now Ray was going to show up in this time of death, and steal the breath away from whatever remained of their lives. Milo dreamed about that last moment on earth when he would be pressed up against that last corner of his existence and from there he would be able to go no further. But before that happened, he wanted to know what it was like to have some of the basic elements of life on earth – like love.

That night he visited with his mother. She said she was honored and amused to be alive and to share in both her own funeral and her son's wedding.

She said, "You must hurry with all your arrangements because I fear I am fading fast. While it will be the most memorable event of my life, it will also be the shortest memory I'll have. When I draw my last breath, I will no longer remember any of it. All my memory banks will be wiped out."

Milo wasn't one hundred percent sure that Samantha was the one for him. Their connection was tenuous at best. And, certainly due to her fragile sexual condition it was a love that was hard to consummate. But sometimes love was a matter of timing. Samantha was there for Milo when New York City was in crisis, and again when the city went dark. She was back now at another pivotal point in his life as his mother was dying. She was a *nick of time* girl. She was his *stand-in* bride. She was his *disaster girl*.

Milo now considered the very real possibility that money and fame might bring him unimaginable female options, perhaps soon women in artistic circles would throw themselves at him, and he would be stuck with her, a simple girl, a bell bottom jean wearing girl, a girl who clenched her knees during love making.

Was this one big mistake?

Chapter Twenty-Five

There was much confusion as Hollywood Becky arrived the next day dressed in designer jeans, with deep black leather luggage, a laptop, iPhone, and some new release chick lit novel. Perhaps she was hoping to buy the rights to it and adapt it for her next project.

She was determined to transform from sleek director of television commercials to a director of films, a quest for her about as elusive as Moby Dick was to Ahab. But still she read those novels, candidates for adaptation, with librarian spectacles on her from California to Gold Haven. Her mother stretched the dying process for three additional days while refusing food or water.

Milo picked up Becky at the airport. As she exited the gate with the other passengers on her flight he was surprised at how his sister resembled Julia Roberts (circa *Pretty Woman*) now, more than ever. She arrived with a respectfully mournful black summer hat, which although solemn sported a festive magenta ribbon.

Milo was well aware that she, just like his art agent, had invested in liposuction and, in her case she had also invested in almost undetectable plastic surgery which ever so slightly widened her eyes and which also made her nose crest in an angle instead of a slight bulbous curve.

Milo was giddy from the roller coaster he had been living on...the long overdue resurgence of his art career, the simultaneous decline and inevitable death of his mother, his impending nuptials, and now the opportunity to see his tight-skinned, impeccably-dressed but still beautiful sister from Hollywood.

"Your plastic surgeon did a spectacular job," Milo said.

"We don't talk about that," Becky answered with a slight turn of her gaze and an accusatory tone. She adjusted her hat which was dangerously close to sliding off her deep black hair.

"Oh, I'm sorry."

"It's cool, I just don't want my surgery to be an issue this weekend. This weekend is about Mom, and it's not about my vanity."

"Oh okay, but it is uncanny what your surgeon was able to do. He had a Midas touch."

"It is a she, and yes, she is a very capable doctor, one of the five best in the country. And although I don't want to talk about this any more, I will tell you that I showed her a photo of me from seven years ago, and she just did some very minor and hard to detect tweaking to make me look like I did then."

"You mean how you looked before 9/11?"

"I guess you could say that."

"Fantastic!" Milo was genuinely impressed, and wondered if it were really that easy to turn back time.

Milo rode in a taxi with his sister Becky, and though she had rewound the clock by seven years, he knew those years had really happened. In those seven years, Milo had mentally cracked, and became the cliché of a tormented artist.

Becky also made a healthy chunk of money directing commercials about foot fungus. The whole ad was a conversation between different sets of bare feet. The bare feet in the thirty second spot engaged in a sophisticated cocktail conversation on the subject of itching, swelling and odor. And in those same years, smooth-skinned Becky did manage to lose a husband because she wouldn't finance his career ambitions.

"You've come along way," Becky said, looking into the mirror from her purse. "You seem so much better."

"Are you talking about me?"

"Yes, of course I am."

"Oh, I thought you were talking to yourself in the mirror."

"No, I was talking about you silly, you seem so much better."

Milo remembered how he was painting a portrait of Vincent Van Gogh one evening in New York City and suddenly stopped everything to re-evaluate his life, to re-shuffle his deck. He just didn't have anything left and couldn't finish the painting. It was the last day he spent in that cockpit sized box in the East Village that had become his sputtering little rocket heading for a crash landing. He pressed his metaphorical eject button, jettisoned into a free fall, and saw rock bottom below. It was as if some greater force told him his days as a street artist were over.

"I really am so proud of you," Becky said. "You have come so far since the last time I saw you."

The last time that she saw him, he was forty pounds heavier and psychotic.

"You are so lucky," she said, "to have Nick behind you. I hope that you've finally learned how to kiss some ass. In any case please bring me up to date on how Mom is doing." Becky's thoughts had a tendency to overlap and then run into each other.

"Well, except for the fact that she is refusing food and water, I suppose okay, for somebody who is on the brink of... Luna has been trying to at least feed her baby food with a turkey baster, otherwise we would have to take her to the hospital."

"My God! I can't believe this is happening."

"And Becky, have you heard the latest news? There is a new plan of action"

"What news? What plan of action?"

"Here's the plan... I am going to be married and mother wants to be here, on earth, to see it, plus she wants to be alive to witness her own funeral." Becky looked at Milo blankly. Milo went on. "It will work this way, I will be having my wedding ceremony in conjunction with her funeral. We are all trying to compress as much as we can into these precious last moments of her life."

"That's absurd. You must be pulling my leg."

"Honest to God truth."

"No way."

"I promise you, I am not lying. This is not a time to play games."

"Well, then, I think you are being mighty selfish with all of this. I really do. You have to learn to let go. Look at me, I am divorced and I am resigned to the fact that Mom won't be around to meet my future husband, whomever he might be. I didn't rush into something quickly trying to piece together my life perfectly, in the nick of time, for Mom to be around to see it. You cannot rush life or death, or marriage."

"Well you seem to be in a mad rush to make a movie and to stop making TV commercials."

"That has nothing to do with Mom dying. I have my goals, but I don't push. You have always pushed. In my opinion that's why you had your nervous breakdown. You are always forcing things to happen on your time table. You have to learn to go with the flow."

"You are the one who has to learn to go with the flow, and the flow is as follows: Mom is dying and I am getting married and we are putting those two elements together. Maybe it is slightly fucked, maybe it is morbid, maybe it is twisted and unorthodox, but that is what is going down."

"Tell me this much, do you even love this girl, what's her name?"

"Samantha."

"Do you love Samantha?"

"Well let me put it to you this way, she has been there for me during the most trying and difficult times in my life. She was there for me in New York when human debris was raining from the sky. She appeared when there was a blackout in New York, and she has come to me now that the most important person in my life is going to leave me forever."

"But you didn't answer my question. Do you love...Samantha?"

"I love her sense of timing."

"A comedian has a sense of timing, Bob Hope had timing, Robin Williams has timing. But we don't go marrying people because they have timing."

"She happens to be here at the right time and place and I am a firm believer in seizing opportunities while they are there for the taking. I have messed up a lot of great chances in my life by being either wishy-washy or too ambitious, and then fluctuating between those two conditions. That's why I am still alone at this ripe old age of forty five. I believe that life can be a lot like surfing, it's all about catching the wave."

"But you've never surfed in your life, you were always too chicken."

"Okay, so it is a lot like body surfing."

"Very funny, Milo." Becky paused to gather her thoughts. "Okay, I apologize. I must say you really know what you want these days. Especially for a person that was once involved in a wipe out and almost drowned. I am continuing with your wave analogy here."

"Thank you. I think."

Milo knew she was referring to his nervous breakdown, so he added, "Just like your nip and tuck, we don't talk about that."

The taxi pulled into their mother's driveway. The lights were all on and the nurse and housekeeper Consuelo, could be seen with Windex and paper towels wiping off the paw marks and dog kiss smears that Moon had left on the front living room window.

As they entered, the house had an eerie chill to it, like in the movie *The Exorcist*. They were keenly aware that somebody was upstairs in an other-wordly state. The downstairs was designated for the living and those planning to stay that way. Becky set down her luggage and Moon scampered to meet her. Moon jumped up on Becky, muddying her jeans with the country and western rhinestones. Borrowing a stunt from watching *The Dog Whisperer* on cable, she straightened her posture and turned away from Moon.

"Now," she said, "the dog knows that I am the alpha in the pack and that I am dominant, and that I will not be subservient to her. Nor will I give her attention nor tolerate her mischievous behavior."

Moon did not watch TV, and being a rebel with claws was oblivious to any form of training. Milo picked Moon up and scratched her belly.

"You must," he said, "go with the flow with Moon. You can't enforce any new trendy form of training technique on her, she is a hippie dog, she has had an alternative form of training, and that is, anything goes."

"Okay, that's fine with me, it's your dog. Listen I would like a glass of water and then I think I will be ready...ready to see Mom."

Chapter Twenty-Six

As Becky and Milo mounted the steps, they heard a moan and a sigh, silence, and then, "POLICE!" being yelled out by a strange voice. Just as their grandmother had ended her days in paranoia, so too was Sonia Sonas. Usually the paranoia struck in the evenings, and the only person so far that had been able to calm her down was Consuelo who sang Cuban and Costa Rican folk songs to her. Milo and Becky rushed upstairs. Consuelo was singing *Guantanamera*, in a surprisingly soothing voice.

Consuelo stood up from the bedside and greeted Becky with a hug. Becky, wrapped her arms around Consuelo, looked cautiously over the nurse's shoulder and saw for the first time what had become of her mother. Her face was gaunt and her skin looked like wax melting over a skull armature. This ghoulish sight instantly reduced Becky to tears.

Without Consuelo's calmative, Sonia Sonas resumed her pleas for police assistance.

"It's okay, Mom, I'm here," Becky said sitting down on the comforter. With her fingers, she brushed the strands of white hair away from her mother's forehead.

"Who knows," Milo said in a whisper, "what sort of horrid visions she sees." He knew all too well how the virtuosic beauty of the world could appear as horrors and delusions, and where small slices of reality had the uncanny ability to morph into visions similar to those depicted in Rodin's *Gates of Hell*.

"Please stop Mom. It's me, Becky, and I flew out to see you. It's okay now. I'm here." Becky genuinely

149

believed her very presence would bring her mother back to sanity.

"Becky, oh Becky. You've come. I'm so sorry, I'm so very sorry you have to see me like this -- dying is so humiliating."

"Don't say that Mom, we all have to die."

"Well as long as we all don't die at once," Sonia said, attempting to muster up some semblance of humor. "But Becky, I'm so glad you've come. This is a wonderful time for Milo. We are really going to go through with it. The wedding will be soon."

"Don't you worry yourself about Milo's wedding, I'm here for you."

Then Sonia said sharply, "Just for me...fuck that. I want this to be a good time. I don't want to be a burden, I don't want your visit to be such a downer. It's going to be fun, it's going to be...Milo when is it going to be? You must hurry, it's so hard for me to hold on, even if I am holding on just for you."

Milo said, "All the arrangements have already been made. It's going to be tomorrow."

Chapter Twenty-Seven

The best part about a wedding for most men is the fact that it is paid for by the father of the bride.

Samantha's father who had first forbidden Samantha from dating Milo, was now changing his tune entirely. He had gotten wind of Milo's pending art world fortune. Samantha, without any prodding from Milo had told her father all about Nick, the collector who had accumulated over one hundred Milo Sonas paintings over the past fifteen years and who now was hell bent on investing in Milo and turning his vast and varied collection into a gold mine.

Samantha had called her father from Gold Haven and expressed the urgency with which she wished to marry Milo, and the immediate need for a caterer. Milo's mother had previously worked for a caterer and it happily cut its fee in half because of its high regard for Mrs. Sonas, despite the rising costs of food, wine and liquor. The discount sealed the deal and Samantha's father expediently wired the money, and sent his blessing. A prior business commitment precluded his attendance. He had always been a father who operated from a distance.

Consuelo had prepared a room for Becky. As she unpacked, Milo sat slumped in a chair exhausted by his own steady determination to make all of the arrangements, while digesting so much sorrow at a time that should have brought him great joy.

Becky then gave Milo a mini-lecture: "You Milo, I must say have a most spectacular Oedipal complex, and if it weren't for the fact that you actually found a girl that likes you, I would say you were treading damn close to Norman Bates territory. You are so lucky I am here, with one divorce behind me, and just coming out of a pretty fucked up fling that I found thanks to the services of match.com, that organization generously offered me another six months free, because I hadn't found the person of my dreams. But I canceled the service. I have had it with internet hook ups."

The man that Becky found on match.com and fell in love with on a Friday night date at Arthur Murray Dance Studio was in fact a professional dance partner on cruise ships. His job was to keep the older ladies entertained. "He was a fucking gigolo," Becky said. "I didn't even know there was such a thing in this day and age. But I am came here to forget all that. It's all about Mom, and I guess you as well. I hope this all works out for everyone involved."

It was to be a simple home wedding and Samantha, being a girl not very prone to pretense was content to choose her wedding gown from the Goodwill Store. She was able to find a classic white dress that made her look like she was wearing a tight fitting parachute that had just touched ground, landing in swirls of white and faded lace.

Samantha:

It was my inner voice that told me I would find what I was looking for there, at that dusty Goodwill. And sure enough there in the back of that color coordinated store I saw a gray double-breasted suit just right for Milo, I knew it was the one, it had pinstripes and an inside label that said Casablanca. He didn't believe me at first and he tried on two other suits, one was too tight at the waist and the other had slacks that were for a giant. He would have to wear stilts to walk in those.

But oh, that gray pin striped double-breasted suit made by Casablanca turned my Milo into a modern day John Dillinger. All he needed was a machine gun prop and he would be ready for action.

I am willing to go through this, for him. I really am. But I have to admit that it doesn't seem real, it seems like everything that transpires between Milo and me, well, it feels pretend, like something that you put on. Our relationship is like a costume, you put it on and you immediately transform into someone new. Like Dillinger and his gal. Bang Bang Bang, let's go through with this lover.

And of course I can't get out of my head the feeling that it is all one big put on to appease his mother in her last moments. What a mama's boy. But who cares, I have always loved mama's boys. They say to watch the way a man treats his mother or a waitress, because sure enough sooner or later that is the way he is going to treat you. I know that Milo will always treat me right, that is if I can get to the bottom of my condition. Shit how are we even going to consummate our marriage if I am so tight. I wish I knew a way that I could relax and stop seeing sex as an attack. I wonder where this all comes from. Probably some deep rooted situation with my father. The thing is, I don't understand it myself.

Chapter Twenty-Eight

Becky had always had a way with plants, animals, children and now, dying mothers.

She took on the turkey baster duties, and quickly got her mother hydrated and fed even if the food had to be put through a blender. The next morning she managed to get her mother out of bed and seated in a wheel chair that she rolled out to the second floor balcony where they basked in summer beams of sunlight.

As for the rushed wedding, the last ingredient missing was the right minister willing to mesh marital vows with last rites.

Becky took but a few minutes to decide the best man for the job, eccentric uncle Allen who lived in the mountains of New Mexico. He had his own stucco home and art gallery featuring erotic wood sculptures that, through extensive sanding and lacquering emphasized the naturally erotic contours of tree trunks and branches. He never altered these found objects, just simply brought out their natural voluptuousness. The viewer of these wood sculptures couldn't help but read sex into these shapes which resembled cleavage, thighs, buttocks and O'Keefe-like vaginal alcoves. He made a modest living out of his woodwork and willingly caught the red eye from New Mexico when he heard that Nick, Milo's dealer/patron would be in attendance.

Milo:

I am nervous about seeing Uncle Allen. I can feel the mounting pressure. I am particularly dreading seeing Ray.

Call me as paranoid as my mother, but it seems pretty clear to me that when I was clinically depressed, when I hardly groomed myself because I was afraid to stand alone in the shower, when I thought the police or some otherworldly gang or some kind modern day vigilante would do me in with a hatchet, well, only then did my family and friends snap into damage control and crisis mode. It seemed it was only when I was in my most flipped-out condition that they were the kindest and the sweetest to me.

And now that I am sponsored by Nick, now that I have this dealer, this owner of a fancy home and a Porsche and a Jaguar, now it seems they have become short with me. Now, I could be wrong about this but I have this theory: they just hate my success, it's killing them, especially Becky and Ray. I know I may be taking this a little too far, but I secretly think that this success is what has eroded my mother's condition and ruined her health. She had been so accustomed to being my caretaker, my spirit guide, my rescuer, the one who has watched over me that I just don't think she can handle the fact that I don't need her so desperately or as much as I did when my life went bust and hit the skids.

And by choosing (and I still insist that somehow deep inside her she is choosing this) to let go of life now, to die now, she subconsciously hopes to make me helpless again. She is forcing me to tie up all my loose ends in a few short days, to do the near impossible. And you know something?...her plan may be working.

On Becky's second night at the house, Milo took a taxi to see her. She was sitting on the sofa in the living room reading a best-seller called *Who The Girl Am I?* It was the story of a navel-gazing GenX woman trying to find herself in New York City after a nasty break up. Becky sought tirelessly for something to adapt.

"You know Milo, you don't see me rushing into marriage so that Mom can see me happy, do you? I spoke to Mom last night and I told her that at this stage of my life, though I may look great, I am frankly quite miserable. Mom was grateful just to hear the truth. You know people can feel the truth, they can sense it, taste it."

"Becky, come off it," Milo said. "I'm sure if you had the opportunity you would want to bring Mom to the premiere of your first feature film, even if you had to wheel her there in her chair."

"Yes, of course I wish she would live long enough to see something like that, but I have learned to let go of that thought pattern. One..has..to..learn..to..let..go."

Now, when people give you that stuff about letting go, it confuses you. It's like that other passive cliché that goes, It will happen when you least expect it. Usually that one pertains to meeting a special someone. These phrases were somewhat prophetic for you because both Samantha's return and the sudden revival of your art career were truly unexpected, and you have to admit that they happened when you let go, when you gave up and hit rock bottom.

Becky held Milo's gaze for a short minute, and then returned to her adaptation candidate.

Milo:
I remember now during my breakdown, all the frustrations of my life reeled before my eyes like a cinematic montage. How could one person survive that many disappointments and close calls?

Who knows, maybe I am some sort of a mama's boy. Maybe she has had too strong a hold on my life and that's why I am choosing Samantha now, while I have the out. I dream at night about all the women that I should have married. Just last night I had a dream that I was Marcello Mastroianni and I was holding hands with my all my exes, the Danish beauty who in turn held hands with the rebellious Brooklyn blonde, who held hands with the girl from Short Hills, New Jersey who held hands with her round conservative sitcom-type Mom and Dad, and they held hands with my Staten Island girl in her Old Navy painters overalls, an erotica book in her pocket, and on it went, down the line, all the short lived romances I had, holding hands, locked in a dance of destiny, all of them celebrating my twelfth hour wedding. Then we took seats on a daredevil carnival ride that lifted us up hundreds of feet then stopped still. We all waited in fearful anticipation, our air bound steel chairs rocking back and forth as we looked down at all the tiny people below. Just then a cable broke and with a whipping sound wrapped itself around the limbs of all my past girlfriends. I shouted to the man at the controls, but he couldn't discern screams of terror from screams of joy. Then he pressed the lever and we dropped into a free fall, and the cable clipped off the limbs of each of my exes, the only girl that went unscathed, un-severed, unwounded was Samantha. And then the limb of the Danish beauty, the manicured left foot of the Queens accountant, the small pale hand of the right wing Republican girl, all those severed limbs shooting through the air, spouting blood. And all I could think about was that this was supposed to be a fun day, a day at an amusement park, a celebration of my marital bliss, not a horror show with all that screaming blending into harmony and keeping time with the

circular monotonous melody of the merry-go-round,
and then boom, swack, boom, I woke up.

"Becky," Milo said. "I guess there are no two ways about it, I am nervous about getting married. Okay, I have the jitters. And although I have hated every minute of being alone, there is a kind of familiar comfort in my extreme loneliness."

Chapter Twenty-Nine

The night that Ray was to arrive at the Gerald Ford airport was a strange one indeed. While Milo and Becky rode in a car service to the airport, there was a spectacular flash storm, a veritable tempest. Raindrops were so thick that they blended together and merged like a 16mm documentary about microscopic cells or atoms. In front of the car was a see-through sheen of water, a moving waterfall. The driver pulled over to the side of the road and the three of them, the driver, Milo and Becky found themselves bursting into nervous, spontaneous laughter as they took in this watery wonderment of nature.

Becky said between chuckles and in a manner of a horror movie narrator, "Ray...has...arrived." She then tried to compose herself in keeping with the somber occasion of her visit to Gold Haven. Looking straight forward at the spectacle, she said, "You know, I am kind of scared to see Ray again. He is such an angry soul. He scares me."

"Me too, I haven't seen him in years. I am surprised he is coming."

"Well, I for one do not forgive him for not showing up when Dad died, or when Grandma died."

"He's the one who has to live with that."

"Sometimes I think he doesn't have a conscience."

"Everybody has a conscience. It comes with the program when we are born."

"Then he was born with that software corrupted. Be prepared Milo to have a sit down pow-wow with Ray. Last time I saw him in LA, he sat me down and went on and on about how he was neglected as a boy. He is still angry at Luna for getting all the attention when she did those soap spots as a child. He said everything was all about Luna. Luna this, Luna that. And then it was all about you and the art you made as a boy."

"I never thought I would be scared of my own brother."

Becky took Milo's hand and held it for a long moment. And then the rain stopped as suddenly as if a fireman had shut down the stream from a hydrant.

The song, *Never Too Much* by Luther Vandross came on over the car service radio, uplifting them both with its breezy grooving retro disco guitar, the driver turned the ignition and got back on the highway. The rest of the ride they were silent.

Milo had a vision of himself standing before his whole family in his Goodwill tuxedo. There was Becky, Ray, Luna, and his half brother Paul and Amelia all circled around the burnt-out big bang that had once been their mother. Then, they were suddenly all children again under the California sun, way back when Father was alive and Grandmother too, back when it seemed "the head of the house" title was shared by Luna and Mother. At the time, Luna and her lucrative TV spots were the bread and butter of the family, and as a young girl she was a force of nature, a perfect child. She ratted on Milo when she caught him getting high. Milo was summoned into his father's office, where the walls were covered by the poster ads of Luna... bare shouldered in Santa Monica, facing the camera with full cheeks and a wink, and a bar of Love soap in her hands. There she was in the flesh, sitting in Milo's father's swivel chair and she said, "Milo, you have a special mind and Mom and Dad and I all agree that you are destroying, as well as distorting, your capabilities with your drug use. What we want you to know most of all is that we know you are stoned."

Milo looked out the car service window as they entered the airport complex. His mind slid back thirty years.

Mother continued where Luna left off. "And so it has been decided that the best course of action is to pull you out of school where you are clearly under the most terrible influence of your truant, foul-mouthed druggie peers."

Milo's father spoke softy, kindly, and under his breath, "Your mind is very different, you have the sort of ability and talent that can't be taught. School will only be a hindrance and a liability to your creative growth. It will push you to fit into a box. And your peers, they will only bring you down to their level."

Now you remember the night they gave you your total freedom. Your sentence and punishment for being high was complete footloose and fancy-free freedom. You had the mornings all to yourself to wake when you pleased and you had Technicolor TV shows to delight in, the colors of Hanna Barbera cartoons, the deep contrasts of Star Trek. In the backyard you could climb the big trees and there you would think about Uncle Allen's wood carvings, trees were shapely women with their legs spread as wide as the girls who did cheer leading. And so you fantasized that you were sitting between the legs of school girls and ladies; and you sucked on the hot Santa Ana breezes and all you could think about was: ha, ha Ray was kept in school while you got out alive. And you imagined a tangled metal Doctor Seuss like mechanism, a complex machine of moving and bending pipes, that stomped and stamped commonness on the brains of other kids, including Ray. You could almost see its rickety clinking and clanking conveyer belt and you could hear its bells sounding off like sirens, sending electric shock waves of terror into the spines of students. And those prison gates, you could see them from the car when your parents drove you past school, they made the building look like a kennel for kiddies, caging Ray like a lost pet at the pound.

As Milo waited at the gate at the Gerald Ford airport, he felt like he was waiting to see a convict, his brother, the former prisoner of education, who after getting a degree in physics from UCLA, chose to become a house painter who painted muddy abstracts in his spare time.

Milo remembered once telling some pretty girl in a New York bookstore that he was an artist and she mysteriously said back to him with far away eyes, "oh, but have you ever painted a white room?"

And Milo answered, "No. But my brother has."

Chapter Thirty

Milo knew that there was something most definitely amiss when he saw his brother exit the gate dressed in light painters' overalls with splatters of white and off-white. He looked like he was wearing a soldier's camouflage for winter warfare. Ray had a wicked smirk on his beard-stubbled face. He embraced Becky, they hardly saw each other although they both lived in Los Angeles, then sized up Milo. "Well you haven't grown any," he said laughing, and as they hugged he whispered into Milo's ear, quite seriously, "it's okay now, it's going to be okay."

And then he said out loud, "Please don't think I've fucking cracked. You see, I caught my flight directly after a house job and I didn't have an opportunity to change. Plus I kinda wanted to freak you all out, but the joke was on me. Airport security checked me out like I was Al Qaeda or something. I was frisked with great determination and I thought for a moment I would be taken into an interrogation room and grilled to see if I had any terrorist leanings. Eventually, they just wrote me off as as a working class nut."

Ray kept talking. "The old lady sitting next to me on the plane, though, she was something. I have to admit she said the nicest thing to me. She said, 'Sir, are you an artist?' to which I answered, 'No, I am just a painter.' Then she said, 'Oh my, a painter, how wonderful, I love paintings, I especially love the impressionists.' 'No, no, no,' I said, 'Ma'am, let me explain, I am a house painter, and I do some abstract dabbling on the side, but I bet you would be just tickled to meet my brother because he is a real living artist.'"

"After I said that, she got kinda uncomfortable but she did ask me all about you and I told her how you have this big time investor art dealer pumping money into your career, and she was thrilled. She asked me why I was flying to Gold Haven, and I said I was coming to a funeral. She said, 'Oh, I am so sorry, who passed?' and I said 'nobody, but my mother is gravely ill.' She said, 'who is the funeral for?' and I said 'for my mother' and she kept saying 'I don't understand.' and I did the best to explain the whole thing to her, a perfect stranger."

"I explained the whole thing to her, how Mom wants to be alive to enjoy her own funeral, and the woman thought I was only joking, and then asked again what I was coming to Gold Haven for and I said to attend the wedding of my artist brother and she smiled and gave me a pinch on the arm for teasing her so much...so that was my surreal flight. Anyhow it never ceases to amaze me how people refuse to accept new concepts into their little box-like brains. And that's why I am so proud of the family that I, I mean we, all come from, because everything is always so skewed with us, so very fucked up."

When Ray arrived it felt like the party had truly begun, the sort that would surely finish at 6:00am in debauchery and recriminations.

Milo was thinking, isn't this what a family reunion is all about? Wasn't it time for celebration, wasn't this supposed to be a tribal ritual about beginnings and endings? The ending of their mother's reign and the beginning of Milo's union with Samantha.

"You can either rent a room at my hotel, or stay at Mom's house with Becky." Milo said to Ray.

"It's okay. I'll just sleep at Mom's house, that's fine with me. This way I can spend some time with Mom first thing in the morning."

"You might get lucky before that," Milo quipped awkwardly, picking up on Ray's light-hearted sarcasm. Then he said, "Mom still has a sleeping disorder, so there is a good chance she will still be up when we get there."

"If you two don't mind," Ray said motioning out the car window, "I am starved."

So they drove through a Taco Bell and Ray ordered eight hard-shell tacos and devoured them quickly. It was amazing to Milo that his brother was able to keep himself so trim and eat like a pig. He had been a child with ample baby fat, a chubby teen and an overweight young adult until his marriage and subsequent estrangement from the family. But his wife changed all that, putting him on an almost carbohydrate free organic diet. Milo had never seen his brother so mean and lean. Ray, pushing fifty now, had the sort of rugged looks that made strangers try to figure out which soap opera he starred in. With physical appeal and standing at six foot two he could have easily become a dominant alpha winner in the corporate world. It was simply preposterous and an almost self imposed flogging of his destiny that he chose house painting as his line of work.

As the taxi drove them out of the Taco Bell parking lot, Ray said, "I know that nobody in this family will forgive me because I didn't fly out to see Grandma or Dad in their death beds, but you have to understand, I didn't want to be a part of the drama that everyone was making out of Grandma's passing. As for Dad, I was complete with him a along time ago. I simply didn't have the need to see him in that condition. But as for Mom, I do have some unfinished business with her.

There is just a bit of tidying up I need to do with you as well, Milo."

Although Ray only said it once, Milo heard his name repeated over and over. *Milo, There is just a bit of tidying up Milo that I need to do with you as well Milo.* And, of course, he heard the Spaghetti Western music playing again.

When the taxi pulled into their mother's driveway all the lights were on. That night the half moon loomed larger than usual as it was magnified by the dense humid night air. Milo's dog was perched on a chair in the front window awaiting their arrival.

Ray's guilt most likely brought him to Gold Haven. His mother had been eager to find out what the hell happened to her oldest son and why had he chosen to extricate himself from the family dynamic. Becky and Milo helped Ray with his duffle bag while cricket chirp sizzled in the air like the sound of electric current. Their mother was having another resurrection and had been up and out of her deathbed since Becky and Milo left for the airport. She was indulging her mania and cleaning the house frenetically. Order and cleanliness had always ruled in the Sonas house, and she would be damned if she would allow herself to be bedridden and leave the house a mess when Ray arrived for his first visit in nearly a decade.

Downstairs Stravinsky emanated from the CD player. Upstairs, a Billy Joel LP played on an ancient hi-fi. *Work'en too hard can give you a heart attack-ack-ack-ack, You oughta know by now*. Sonia Sonas was oblivious to both sounds and stood in the kitchen loading the dishwasher. When she saw Ray enter, she managed to muster up some other-wordly energy and tearfully exclaim, "Well I'll be God-damned, it really is you Ray" in her best impression of Katherine Hepburn playing Mary Tyrone in *Long Day's Journey into Night.*

Upstairs the record was skipping and the stylus skated across the vinyl record to its last groove, then thumped repeatedly. Milo thought quickly of the thunderstorms that foretold Ray's arrival at the airport and darted upstairs to turn off the album. Their mother abhorred the stringent sound of CDs and still treasured her record collection.

Ray continued the theatrics. "And, yea, there is no doubt that you are the mythic archetype known as Mother." His delivery was blunt and listless, like an actor in a high school play or like Keanu Reeves in his philosophical surfer mode.

"And you, Ray, are what is commonly known as my first born son."

"Mom," Becky said, interrupting the dramatic reunion, "what are you doing up and out of your bed all by yourself cleaning up like this. Where is Consuelo? This her her job."

"I sent her out for wine and groceries," Sonia said, leaving the theater antics behind.

"She is not supposed to leave you in the house all alone. What the hell were you thinking?"

"Hey, I am her boss and ultimately she must do what I say. It's my insurance that pays her salary."

"But nobody would be here if you fell flat on your ass and broke your hip." Becky changed her tone and tried to throw some humor into the moment.

"What if, what if, whatever... the fact is, there is no way I would let myself miss out on the pleasure of seeing my oldest boy, and for the first time in ten years. Or the joy in seeing my youngest boy get married. Or to hear everybody sing my praises at my own funeral. I am mighty curious as to what exactly you squirts will say in your sobbing tributes to yours truly."

At that moment Consuelo arrived through the back door, with wine wrapped in a brown bag, and two plump grocery bags. She slid into the room, mime-like, took out the wine, and hunted for an opener.

In impressive Spanish Becky reprimanded Consuelo and ordered her never to leave her mother alone in the house again. Consuelo apologized and said she had only just been to the local liquor store which was three minutes away, and that she did so in honor of Señor Ray's arrival.

"Gracias," Ray said. He had a rudimentary understanding of Spanish having disastrously once apprenticed with a Mexican relative who was an artist, poet and a mind blowing drug abuser and alcoholic. Sarcastically, he added, "I am especially honored that, because of my arrival, my mother's life was put in jeopardy for a bottle of cheap wine. But come on Mom, you can't drink wine, you haven't had any food or water for two days."

"Ray, I am many decades over twenty one, and I don't take orders from you. I have my rights. In fact they may be my last rites, ha ha, and they are that I can drink about as much as I damn please. So please, fill-er-up."

And so four glasses of tart red wine were poured. Becky and Milo sipped theirs slowly, while Ray and his mother gulped their wine down in a near-guzzling. It only took Ray but five minutes before he downed two more glasses of wine and began to blush and gush like any repenting prodigal son should.

"Listen Mom, the thing is, I know that you are disappointed in what I have done with my life. I know I cost you a lot of money, like when you bailed me out of jail."

"You know," Milo said interrupting Ray's tipsy heartfelt confession, "I heard about that through the grape vine, but I never got a clear idea of what exactly went down."

"Oh, I know the story," Becky chimed right in, "Ray was caught breaking and entering into an apartment in his own building. Right? Didn't they find you in your neighbor's apartment, cash on your belly, asleep on the couch? The neighbor called the cops and you got thrown in jail. Mom had to bail you out to the tune of ten grand. You called her crying that if you didn't get bailed out you would miss out on work and your ass would be fired."

"And I was more than happy to be of service," Sonia said, her voice like the creak of a rusty old door.

"That story," Ray bellowed, thumping his fist on the kitchen table, causing the salt and pepper shakers to quiver and a low tide wave within the wine glasses, "that story is a total crock of horse shit. Okay, so there is a slight grain of truth in it. I was shit-faced that night. I'd spent the evening in a strip club, that's right a titty bar and a certain sweetheart there gave me some powerful body shots of Jagermeister. It felt like I was a vampire sucking the alcohol straight out of her skin. When I bit her, they kicked me out. I ended up with a bloody lip, I'm not sure how I got it, but I should have sued the shit out of them." Ray went on, tipsy in his delivery, "Okay, so I walked the two or three blocks home, vision blurry, puking perhaps once or twice, some blood in it too. Got back to my place and find my key is jamming in my door, so I jimmied the lock with my jack knife. I was good at that, it was like stealing kisses, ha ha. The lock was a cinch and I was in right away. So I search the place, see. Shit I'm sounding like Edward G. Robinson in *Little Caesar*. Then I search my place for Advil, extra strength, because I felt like my brain was spilling out of my skull, who knows I probably had a concussion, but then I gave up and passed out on the couch. I must have only been asleep a couple of minutes when all of a a sudden I wake up to find a cop jabbing me with his night stick and telling me I have a right to remain silent and all that jazzy TV cop show shit, and they take me in and I don't go easy. I keep yelling at 'em, 'What the hell are you cops doing in my apartment without a warrant?' That's what happened."

"Okay, enough already," Becky said, her voice rising. "Don't tell us that you didn't know that was not your apartment, because nobody here is buying that crap."

Ray now looked perplexed, "I swear to God that was my apartment, the whole thing was a set up."

"Your apartment was next door, you had broken into and ransacked your neighbor's place."

After a moment Ray relented, settled down and spoke softly, "It was an honest mistake, I thought I was home...that's right I had the wrong apartment, the wrong door. I wanted door number one and I got door number two. I really only wanted to find my Advil. Is that such a crime?"

"The only mistake you made, "Becky added, "was drinking in the first place. Ray you a have problem. You are an alcoholic."

"Okay, okay, so my name is Ray and I am an alcoholic. But Becky you shouldn't be the one to point your finger. You should focus on your own sobriety, Miss whiskey nightcap girl."

Milo wondered how they knew so much about each other. It was like no time had lapsed at all.

"I have it under control. I don't wake up in strangers' apartments. I don't hunt for Advil in bathrooms that aren't mine."

"Okay, touche to you."

"Touche to both of you, now stop it," their mother said, mustering up the strength to yell almost as loudly as she did when they were kids. "I've had enough of your bickering. These are the last evenings I will ever have. Can you understand that? It's bad enough for me that I will have to die in the summertime, but I guess it's just as well. I don't think I could tolerate another Michigan winter. The winters here have been killing me and so are the two of you right now!" Sonia Sonas was drunk. "It's bad enough to know that one of my sons lives in a flop house Downtown, living next door to rapists and crack heads. And, it has broken my heart Ray to know that you still have only hatred for us, your own family, your own blood. What did we ever do to you to make you hate us so? Tell me what! And with your education, to choose to be...a house painter."

Ray retorted, unable to maintain the half-pleasant facade he arrived with, "Oh, that's rich. Don't you get it? You all left town, you just moved on with your lives, picked up to New York and left me, just as I was going to attend UCLA. It was as if I was a leper, it was as if I was going to catch TB on campus and it was contagious. You never came out to visit, even on the holidays.

"Oh come on, Ray." Becky said, "Don't you think you are exaggerating just a wee bit. We were just leading our lives. Right, Mom? Milo needed to be in New York."

Their mother was tiring, and she was angry. It seemed as though her larynx was losing its elasticity. Her voice sounded dry, haunted, ill, but willful in its determined raspiness, "Look you guys, I never had a chance to go to school at all. You kids had all the breaks. I was told to go to work and give seventy five percent of every nickel I earned to my parents."

"Okay, so that was how it was for you," Milo said, a crack in his voice as he quickly regressed to boyhood. "But there was no reason for you to hand the same lot down to your kids, didn't they ever tell you that every new generation is supposed to have it better than the one before it."

"We pulled you out of school Milo because you were special, you were an artist."

Ray joined in Milo's complaint: "Look what being an artist did to Milo. When the streets of New York finally spit him out, he had nothing to fall back on. He had to come here with his tail between his legs. He's uneducated, but at least he has the dignity to live on his own, even if it is in a real dump of a hotel." Ray was smiling. "I do salute you for that Milo, But look at you. In the end you are still living in a hundred square foot box, except it is not in Manhattan, it is in nowhere, Michigan."

"This isn't the end. And, I won't be living that way for long. In the fall my art is going to auction, and things are going to change."

"At least you hope so," Ray teased.

"No Ray, I know so." Milo straightened his posture, puffed out his chest with pride and stared straight into Ray's eyes.

"All right, all right, enough," Becky said. "We are all just speculating. Why don't we all stop living in the past and in the future and let's start living in the present, in the here and now. Look at the sky outside, the way the moonlight shines on the tree."

The four of them glanced out the kitchen window and indeed the moon was illuminating a thick, giant, slingshot shaped, spread-legged tree. Ray sneered. "That actually looks like some of Uncle Allen's tree erotica. Doesn't it? Doesn't it look like that bitch tree wants it bad?"

174

Chapter Thirty-One

The erotic tree sculptor himself and his wife arrived the very next morning. Uncle Allen had long white hair, a white beard and a finely etched face that made him look like a weathered Kris Kristofferson. His skin was dark from exposure to the New Mexico sun. He looked like a carved totem pole Indian that one sees in a cigar shop. He eagerly hugged Milo. With Uncle Allen came cousin Edna, her husband, the Santa Fe realtor and their two children who were clearly perplexed by the concept of the wedding slash funeral combo. Perhaps they were spooked by the prospect of the ceremony taking place in a cemetery. Children do not need spoon fed explanations. They just need to experience the moment like an adult and decide for themselves what to think.

They had arrived on a morning flight, and the ceremony was that very afternoon. Nobody was going to take any chances and waste time. Sonia Sonas was going fast and it was to be the biggest, strangest party that this family had ever thrown. The fact of Milo getting married in itself was a miracle. Added to that, was the weirdness of Mrs. Sonas attending her own funeral.

Samantha's father had decided to fly in at the last moment. He was a solemn, short man of few words. He looked roughly the same age as Milo, which made them both uncomfortable. Carly, the girlfriend that Samantha wanted to set Vincent up with finally showed up at the bus station and took a taxi to the house. She was a mean spirited girl of Polish descent, built low to the ground, but with a strong gymnast's body. She chain-smoked and was prematurely bitter for her age of twenty three, complete with her furrowed brow. But she also was very sexy, in that "mean girl" way.

Carly was pissed off that the hitch hiking didn't pan out and that she had been coerced into such a long bus trip. She and Vincent met for coffee, but Pablo showed up too. His coal black eyes captivated her. He said nothing more to Carly but, "You have cigarettes, you have brown eyes, both things that I love in a woman."

She broke a smile at his flippant comment. Her response to Pablo visibly hurt Vincent since it had been the first time that this new visitor, intended for Vincent, smiled. And then Pablo added insult to injury when he said something unnecessarily cruel, "Vincent, why do you have that expression on your face, like your mother just died?"

The statement brought Milo down. Samantha took his hand and assured him, "He's just being an ass. Your mother is still here, yes, she's still with us, still here to share this special day. Just don't listen to him, he's being mean spirited. He is a mean spirit after all, and though he is known the world over, his renown can never bring him back to life, and he knows it."

"May I talk to you for a minute?" Milo said to Pablo.

The two of them had a talk outside while Vincent and Samantha and Carly looked on, but couldn't hear the words. The two girls watched through the glass window, as Milo's mouth moved and Picasso gestured back. Milo was telling Pablo to just cool it, this was Vincent's moment. "Look Samantha managed to get her friend to come all the way out here to make sure that Vincent could have a little fun."

"But what is the use in all of this?" Pablo said, striking a match to yet another cigarette and blowing the smoke into Milo's face. "Didn't anybody ever tell you that it's no use, we cannot consummate. He won't be able to feel a thing. Not her touch, not her kiss, *nada*, and if she were to reach for him to even stroke his arm, he would feel nothing. It's too late for us now, we are nothing but dead artists. You should be more concerned with yourself. Listen to me closely Milo. I am not sure how to put this except to say that now that there is a possibility of things happening for you, of you being a real famous artist just as I was, you have to make sure to feel everything, as you go through with it, try to remember everything, every sensation. You have one more new beginning in your life, one more half of life, don't blow it by moving through it too quickly or too blindly."

"Okay, Pablo. I hear you. Now let's go inside, but please be nicer to Vincent."

The Sonas family had always known how to throw a good party. There was a time when that was all they did. During Milo's childhood, the crazed "weekend get-togethers" of his mother's extended Latin family were extremely distracting to Milo and also proved most detrimental to his early formal education. And this was before his so-called home schooling. How can a child focus on academia when on a Friday night the family's pet chimpanzee swung from the curtains to the living room chandelier or landed on the Formica table eating ravishingly from the *arroz con pollo*? How could he focus on algebra on a Monday morning with memories of a weekend in which it was okay for the kids to have shots of tequila administered to them by Uncle Allen? What about the way that they joked about the possibility of an apocalypse during the cold war years? When it seemed the big bomb would end it all? How can a kid concentrate on anything but anarchy when the end of the world could come at any given moment? What about the hootenannies where their hippie friends sang songs to protest the war in Vietnam, or songs in favor of the pill, like the song that Uncle Allen sang while strumming a six string: *I'm not fucking worried about fucking anymore cause my girl got that little pink pill from the Pharmacy store.*

And the other song he hollered in his speak song fashion: *I want to be alive to see my funeral day, I won't want to miss all the cryin, no there's no way, so while I'm still six feet above, throw me a party so I can feel the love, yeah while I'm still alive and kicking. I want to feel the love...*

That song was a-strummin' and a-hollorin' through Milo's head all day long. And he realized that the memory of that song was the root of his concept to create this double bill wedding and funeral.

Milo had been written off as un-marriagable just like his cousin Little Glen because he was forty five and still living in the house where his mother had died. Little Glen was a fellow aging bachelor, and he hadn't swept, mopped, cleaned, dusted or organized that ranch style home, near the freeway in Los Angeles in twenty years. Somehow it seemed those that were born in the Kodachrome and Technicolor sixties couldn't get it together and couldn't get it on with women now in the information age.

For Milo it was all pretty simple, he just couldn't afford to get married. Sure, girls of a certain age (those under twenty two) would find it novel and fun to sleep with him a couple of times in his East Village cave during his lucky street selling days. But then, when the sales would run dry (it happened to even the best most diehard street artists) the girls would find it incomprehensible that he would not whip out the "help wanted" ads and find himself some steady work. But no, Milo would keep hitting the streets during hard times, even during the subzero dregs of February. Why? Well, because a street artist never knows when they might run into a high roller. Those were the "catches" who might come to his studio and purchase the big canvases for big money or commission him to create something for them, paying half up front and the other half upon completion. But sometimes they never came and he'd hit rock bottom living off the collection of coins that had built up in a jar. He would take that jar to the CoinStar machines at the supermarket and get a voucher for cash. Once he cashed in one hundred and ten dollars in coins and he took his girlfriend to Little Italy and they spent it all in one night. In those frugal days and nights it never even occurred to him to go to the grocery store and stock up, nor did it occur to him to invest in a simple hot plate and cook for himself and his women.

Samantha had told her father Milo's stories of hardship and he had such an unfavorable opinion of Milo that he refused to condone or to fund the ceremony beyond the discounted catering. The only reason he flew out was because he had heard about the financial hope on Milo's horizon. Nick picked up the slack and paid for everything *Carte Blanche*. The main costs were a tent for the wedding, reserving a grave sight at the Kalamazoo cemetery and quickly arranging for a freshly dug grave and a limestone grave stone carved with the words: *Sonia Sonas lies here, the beloved mother of Ray, Paul, Luna, Amelia, Becky and Milo. She has watched over them like a spirit guide and an angel.*

Milo felt that the phraseology and the whole *spirit guide* business was directed solely at him.

After all, he was the one who brought her the most worry. He was the one she loomed over the longest. His was the studio she cleaned and organized. She had been there for him after his big bang nervous breakdown, even administering him an enema when he had cried out one night in paranoia, stammering that "they have sewn my asshole shut, they want me dead." He had become convinced that the government wanted him to die from the inability to shit. That they thought he was loitering on earth because he was one of those lazy coffee shop casualties who wandered the earth in the afternoons. Because he didn't contribute to the monetary system...that they want to kill him so that he could be another god-damned dead artist!

All that was over with now, thank god and it was wonderful and bright outside. It was a particularly humid, muggy afternoon and his cousin Little Glen stood in his new shiny suit appearing both sinister and cute. A scattering of Nick's friends flew in, they stood out from the crowd in that they looked current, up-to-the-minute and trendy like they belonged in Cannes or Monaco or New York. And then there was Milo's mother, wheel chair bound again, but looking radiant in a stark red dress. Samantha who had dyed her Goodwill wedding dress black for this day of duality was wondering after seeing Mrs. Sonas's red dress if she shouldn't have just left the wedding dress white after all.

Uncle Allen was joined by a minister, Dan Boswick, who was chosen by Luna (and therefore was well versed in alternative ceremonies). He stood among the gravestones, metal folding chairs and the make shift wooden trellis decked out with roses, and managed an expression that was both somber (for the funeral) and delighted (for the wedding). Samantha mostly hung around her single bridesmaid Carly, who dressed in

Gothic chic. She looked lovely and devilish, as if she had stepped out of an Anne Rice novel.

Milo had wanted Samantha to wear red this day, but she refused, she didn't want to look like a woman of ill repute from a bad western.

It is always advisable to marry young, so that those in attendance do not resemble bingo players or losers from a thirty year high school reunion. All together a smattering of about fifty people showed up, mostly middle aged and above. Samantha and Carly who both wore reef flowers in their hair gave the ceremony a much needed injection of youth. Samantha and her friend supplied the hope. Milo and his family supplied the gloom. Becky and Amelia's friends seemed appropriately and understandably bewitched as to whether they should be bereaving and weeping, or well wishing with tears of joy running down their cheeks. Then over a makeshift sound system came the Carpenters' song, *We've Only Just Begun*. This blatantly sentimental song offered a young Milo the false promise of what love might feel like. But Milo was never able to achieve the emotion created by this sappy masterpiece. When the song concluded and Milo and Samantha had finished walking around the grave, the minister with his braided hair and beard began his oratory: "We are here, brothers and sisters, friends and neighbors, to celebrate the life and death of Sonia Sonas, as well as to share in the union of her son Milo with Samantha. Two disparate events it seems, but perhaps not at all. There are, I believe three hallmarks of life's journey, birth, marriage and death. And we have two of them embodied here. We have Mrs. Sonas who admittedly is in the last days of her life..."

"Last day, not days!" Mrs. Sonas managed to yell out. "I ain't gonna last days, believe you me."

There was a smattering of laughter and the minister continued the proceedings as planned. "Okay, as we celebrate the last day of Mrs. Sonia Sonas, we also come together to witness the marriage of her youngest son Milo to Samantha Tristan. Mrs. Sonia Sonas has expressed the desire to share these last moments with those who are nearest and dearest. In so many funerals those who are gone, do not get to share in the bereavement of their death. But with Mrs. Sonas we are honored to be able to have her have that rare, almost unheard of chance this summer afternoon. And now some words from Luna Sonas."

Luna stepped up to the microphone and told her mother that she loved her, and thanked her for always coming over and cleaning her house. And that was all she said, because she began to cry, but then her cry turned into laughter as she said, "This is such a schizophrenic day."

Next, Becky's speech went as follows, "When I was a child, I saw my sister Luna's commercials on the TV set, commercials for soap, they were my earliest education in advertising. I have always wished to be more than just an ad girl and to make a film of my own but it turns out after five years of trying that I have to accept who and what I am. I am Becky Sonas and I am in advertising. I am a corporate tool, a hack. But there is a happy ending here because in a way I have now come full circle, I have been asked to work for the same Love Soap brand that Luna was a spokeschild for all those years ago. Now, when I got this account I was completely blocked as to how I would approach the thirty second spot, and then it hit me, I would ask Luna to be featured in the ad. It is obvious when we look at Luna and at my mother as well, that they still both share the most wonderful skin. And Luna was kind enough to say "yes". Okay so I won't be directing the remake of *Citizen Kane* any time soon, but mother, I wanted to share the news with you, because it will be a chance for Luna and me to work together again. As for Milo's wedding, well I am sure you have all noticed the one man crew with a video camera in his hand, well that is my gift to Milo. This wedding-funeral will be captured in high definition video so that Samantha and Milo can treasure this moment forever and the world can watch it on YouTube."

It was then that Milo noticed this inconspicuous cameraman with a mini-cam in his palm, so small it could have been a cell phone.

"This is my friend Brian," Becky said, "and he is great at capturing real moments. He has the most amazing ability to make himself invisible, and so please everyone, continue to be yourselves. No need to mug for the camera. Okay?"

Mother was beginning to tear up.

Ray declined to share his feelings about mother, he was more focused on taking swigs from his white wine spritzer.

The minister took center stage again and cued Uncle Allen. He called Milo and Samantha to stand before him. "We are also gathered here today, to join in matrimony Milo Sonas, and Samantha Bella Tristan as well as honor the life of my sister Sonia Sonas." And he said, "if anybody has anything to say against it, speak now or forever hold your peace."

Brian the cameraman panned the crowd with that tiny secret agent styled lens.

Milo and Samantha faced the crowd and nobody spoke. Uncle Allen smiled, then said, "I now pronounce you husband and..."

"IT'S A FUCKING JOKE! That's what this whole thing is!" A voice heckled out these words and all heads turned to discover that it was coming from a very drunk Ray, who now had a silver flask of vodka in his hand. He was himself again, and began his destructive reign of terror. "My dear little brother Milo, always wanting, needing, craving attention. God forbid that at the end of her life Mother should have a moment in the sun all to herself. No, it also has to be a moment that is all about you, and your stupid little union."

"Please don't do this now Ray." Mrs. Sonas said, but her voice was gurgling, full of phlegm, and had no volume or power. In fact the only person that heard her utterance was the ever so timid Consuelo, and there was nothing she could do about it, considering she had barely understood what was taking place that afternoon. The only thing she knew for sure was that Ray was drunk. She knew drunk when she saw it. Her ex-husband destroyed their marriage when she was nineteen all in just a few months with alcohol abuse.

Ray continued, spittle coming from his mouth, "He thinks he is so damn special, who the fuck does he think he is, Pablo Picasso or Vincent Van Gogh?"

This statement made Pablo and Vincent stiffen their posture. Pablo in particular looked like he was ready to retaliate. He mumbled to himself, "Bastardo!"

"This guy," Ray said pointing rudely at Milo "never even accepted our father. No, ever since I can remember he was always telling anybody that would listen that Picasso was his real father, and Van Gogh was his godfather. Milo is living a dream, a dream put into his head by that fool called Nick, who got all his money from an old man he wasn't even related to. Now Milo thinks he can "de-value" our mother by upstaging her last rites by marrying one of his little coed girlfriends. Samantha, you stupid bitch. You don't even understand why he is so hot on you? It's because you are a university girl. See my kid brother got short changed out of a higher education and he has developed this fetish for any girl that holds text books against her breasts. That, and in addition to the fact that he is a pedophile."

"Please not now," Mrs. Sonas muttered in Spanish and Consuelo, whose intuition told her things were really askew now, took Mrs. Sonas' skeletal hands and held them warmly in her soft, dark-skinned palm.

"I know what you all think of me," Ray whined, now truly indulging in the awkward spotlight of attention. "You are all thinking, oh, he's the one in the family who paints houses, while Milo, well Milo is the *artiste*."

Milo, dressed uncomfortably in a suit that was still brittle from its starchy dry-cleaning, called out "Ray, what is wrong with you?. Why do you always have to ruin perfectly good moments? It seems to me like you didn't learn jack shit at UCLA. I didn't realize you had a Masters in assholeology."

"Look at our mother," Ray said, nearly crying and pointing again. "She looks like she is over one hundred years old and she is only seventy um..."

"You don't even know how old she is," Milo said. " She is seventy nine, you fucking loser." Milo was on his feet, heading toward Ray as Vincent, (who was invisible to the guests) put his hand on Milo's shoulder to settle him down.

But Ray would not stop. "The last few years have really aged her. I am speaking of the last few years since your oh so convenient nervous breakdown. You have been like a festering cancer to her health. She has worried sick over you for twenty years. She busted her ass covering your ass when you were down and out in New York, you asshole! You used to call her twenty times a day, wearing her out. You were always moaning that this time your career was really over, boo hoo, boo hoo. You didn't get to be Picasso. You fucking destroyed her with your negativity. You are still killing her."

Both Ray and Milo took a breath at the same time, they were blood brothers after all and even in a dispute they were still in synchronicity with the other's biology. Milo turned to Samantha and gave her his wedding ring in it's tiny padded box. Samantha was sobbing.

Now Ray was considerably bigger than Milo. There was no doubt he was Goliath to Milo's David. But a lifetime of anger had built up in both of them.

Milo's nephew Donny, though only sixteen, was beefier than both of them and he was not too happy about this out of town brother messing things up for his favorite uncle. And Donny stood still as he watched Milo stride right up to Ray. Donny was tempted to beat the shit out of Ray himself, but then again he thought it would be better to let Milo do it himself. Donny called out, "Beat the hell out of him. You know you can do it Milo!"

Milo moved toward Ray feeling a strength in his body, a stiffening in his spine. Years of sporadic contact with his brother brought this dissonance to a head. Mountains of resentment, each fragmented and distinct, slight, and aggravation flickered before him. And Ray, not sensing the intensity of Milo's anger, continued egging him on. "So, are the two of you going to live happily ever after in a halfway house? Is that the plan?"

Nick's inner reactors were being engaged for he was just now planning to cover first and last month, plus security on a loft on the lower East side of Manhattan for Milo and Samantha. This was to be Milo's chance to begin again, to have his dignity again, and more than that, to flourish in the very city that almost destroyed him. Nick was planning to facilitate the chance for Milo to come full circle. Nick believed that New York was where Milo belonged and he was not about to have some drunk, bitter, and envious bully of a brother bring down the very foundation of artistic self esteem that he was spending tens of thousands of dollars to bolster.

Nick had traveled with a few of his associates to Gold Haven to be there for Milo, and this caustic scene was hardly what he expected. At five foot seven inches and hundred and thirty five pounds, Nick was not a formidable presence but he was nervy from having been sitting uncomfortably on a particularly hard folding chair, two rows behind Ray and, if he were to rudely reach forward with his long arms he could grab Ray by the lapel. Instead he simply stood up and towering over the seated crowd bellowed, "Excuse me, sir, just one moment please. I have a great respect for your family but I have a vested interest in Milo. I happen to know he's been through a lot in his life to get to where he is and to go where he is going. And I, for one, give him a lot of credit. You Ray have to get hold of yourself now, and simmer the hell down."

Some young upstart who was at the controls for the sound system, thought he might contribute to maintaining the peace by cuing a song that was Mrs. Sonas' favorite, *Imagine* by John Lennon as sung by *American Idol* runner-up David Archuleta. It was supposed to play at the end of the ceremony, but it came on now in the middle of this showy disagreement. The loud volume silenced the crowd. And when Archuleta sang: *Imagine all the people living life in peace Yoo Hoo hoo-oo-oo* Ray raised his fists in a most old fashioned manner. He was putting up his dukes and walking up the aisle, and he resembled, in his ill fitting suit and bowie tie an illustration of a turn of the century boxer. He now stood face to face with Milo. Milo raised his fists as well.

When they were children these two brothers cloaked their fists in pillows and would fist fight with those cumbersome soft pillows as boxing gloves to soften their blows.

Ray said, "Well, little brother, it's about time you fight your own battle. It's about time you stood up for yourself."

Consuelo could now feel Mrs. Sonas' hands go cold. She was able to follow the silent film laid out in front of her. "Que espanto!" Consuelo found herself saying when Ray pushed forth the first blow. This instantly bloodied Milo's nose. Milo retaliated with a punch that struck only air. Ray followed with an undercut to the ribs, that not only knocked the air out of Milo, but triggered a collective gasp from the onlookers that was inaudible to the crowd because of the loud music.

Milo lunged at Ray and they both got locked in a wrestler type hold that resembled the embrace of two world federation fakers.

The two brothers stood locked in that embrace, twisting about. Then they broke apart and Milo looked shaken. Physical contact with men was not his thing. He looked rattled, his face was red and he was sweating. Ray came at him with a torrent of punches. Ray gave Milo a knee kick to the groin, followed by two karate chops to the wind pipe. Milo doubled over in pain. Nick spontaneously took on the roll of referee and called out, "Hey, those were some cheap shots, now cut it out."

Milo fell to his knees and Ray walked slowly to his younger brother and then broke every semblance of decency when he kicked his brother directly in the face, knocking Milo off his knees face first into the grassy grave yard.

At this point, Paul, their half-brother got up and tried to restrain Ray saying, "Come on man, what do you think you are doing, this is Milo's day, why do you have to fuck it up like this?"

"Lay off me, Paul." Ray said overpowering Paul's effort to restrain him, and it wasn't long before he got Paul in a choke hold, "Today is Mother's day, not Milo's day!"

Although Paul was in a choke hold he managed to eke these words out: "Look, it's Milo's day too, it was decided. I think what is pissing you off the most is that it is not your day. It is never your day!"

"Like I said, it's Mom's day," Ray insisted, still keeping Paul in a tight grip.

Now, Paul was speaking softly, confidentially so that their mother could not overhear, "Listen man, for all we know this could be her last one, so why don't you just cool it?"

"Do you really think this could be it ...for her?" Ray asked.

"I really think so, just look at her.."

They both looked towards their mother who seemed confused by what she was seeing.

Now Ray spoke as loudly as a caterer announcing that the wedding buffet was being served, "Milo killed her, she has made herself sick with worry over him. He did this to her."

"Fuck you, Ray." Paul said, drooling from the choke hold.

Ray let go of Paul who dropped to the ground.

Bloodied, winded, humiliated, and now dressed in a torn lawn-stained gray suit, Milo recovered enough to slowly get up on his feet. Ray let him be.

Milo said, "There has always got to be somebody or something that fucks with my life. I guess this proves my theory that there is no such thing as a perfect moment. At least there never has been for me."

Milo, unexpectedly found himself emotionally regressing as if in a dream where one stands on a stage in one's briefs, or like one who must speak in front of class in urine soaked slacks. It was a fight or flight situation. He sensed that maybe back hundreds of generations ago perhaps in his primitive ancestry he was one of those pathetic primates who fled from an opponent, be it a Tyrannosaurus Rex or a meddlesome monkey man. He was a runner not a fighter.

Milo discovered himself running through the graveyard. He was a runaway. Running away from the living, weaving his way through the granite postal addresses of the dead. But nobody wrote letters to these stone mailboxes, these underground coffin condos. As he ran around them, and sometimes in his confusion jumped over them, all he knew was that he was going away. Where he was running to, at the moment, did not matter.

As he moved, he remembered how all his life his mother had always claimed that graveyards were a total waste of space, she called graveyards, "the ego trip of the dead." Milo ran around the large stone monuments which were guarded by statue angels with blind marble eyes. The sculptor in him couldn't help but notice the stiffness of American statue work. It reminded him of how he, as a teenager had approached a sculpture gallery on Park Avenue. He came on strong and aggressive and managed to get a few unscheduled moments with the gallery owner. He showed this very thin woman photos of his early busts made of clay and his unbridled confidence and with an almost abrasive salesmanship humored the gallerist. After examining his works at her vast white desk, she told him that his Rodin-esque busts had what she called "real juice" but warned him there was limited hope of financial success for a budding sculptor in this day and age. She said quite frankly, "Sculpture reminds people of death, and it's the fault of all those damn monuments in graveyards."

As Milo ran, he knew he was running away from more than just the burden of having a brutally envious and emotionally poisonous older brother, he was also running from the imminent and inevitable loss of his spirit guide, his always watching, always kind mother. He knew in his heart that, even if he married now, it was unlikely he would live long enough to know Samantha longer than he had known his mother. So many recent summer nights he had found it hard to sleep knowing the truth. That there would soon come the fall, a time his mother loved because of the reddening of the leaves, and the chilly breezes which made the trees shiver. But she might as well die now because all that she would now conveniently miss after the falling of the leaves would be the freezing wind and the white dandruff of winter snow. But why couldn't she behold one last fall? God, could you grant her one more Autumn, he found himself thinking. Even though he was not so sure about God either. But just about now would be a good time to discover and believe in him.

Then of all absurd things he discovered that he was not running alone. On the contrary, the whole congregation of friends and family were up and running after him. They were right behind him all along, but because he never looked back over his shoulder, he was totally unaware that he was being followed so devoutly and at the head of the formally dressed herd was Ray. This was not good.

Milo found himself running backwards, amazed as he was by the sight of everyone, including Samantha, who was holding her white high heel shoes and running barefoot to him.

It occurred to him then that he had also been running from her. How could he tie the knot now? Why now, when he was on the verge of an opportunity to enjoy the sensual fruits of all the dues he had paid for half his life. Surely when the galley shows came, the long limbed models would soon follow, and the aristocratic daughters of wealthy collectors, and society debutantes, and night life celebutantes, the sensual undergraduates, those sexy liberal art majors all wishing to get to know that elder statesmen of the art world, that veteran of sidewalk selling who had become the king of the contemporary art market, Milo Sonas. Why marry now when all the money and all the fucking was on its way, why commit now to just one girl?

But then he reminded himself that he was attempting to simulate completeness for the sake of his good as dead mother.

Samantha! Ray! Nick!

He could see them all running at him, Becky, Amelia, Paul. They were gaining on him too.

Ray was way ahead of everyone else, and he looked like he was still festering with anger. He called out to Milo, as he caught up, "Didn't you know Milo that I'm not going to quit this until you are dead?"

Milo stopped in his tracks at that statement, he just couldn't run any longer He would feel too vulnerable with his back facing his violent brother.

Now, his brother stood before him again.

"Don't you know what wonderful things will happen for your art when you are dead. Most artists only get famous when they die."

Ray shoved Milo. Milo didn't budge, his posture straight, he wanted to at least try to be invincible.

Milo said, "And if you kill me, what happens to your life? It is ruined."

DEAD ARTIST

"On the contrary I gain fame and notoriety as the brother who killed you. They will say in the history books, Ray Sonas, was the guy who killed that famous artist Milo Sonas."

"Is that what you want to be known for?"

"I have no choice, what the hell else will I be remembered for? I mean nobody cares about a guy like me. Nobody cares that I am such an efficient wall and ceiling painter or that I have no need for canvas tarp. Who cares that I never drip paint when I work? Nobody. Who would give a shit about about a guy like me? I'm just a house painter and you are an artist."

"Funny, a painter who does not drip." Milo said trying to get Ray to smile, "I am a messy painter myself. Bravo to you."

Ray was not humored, he shoved his brother again, and this time Milo lost his balance and fell backward. But strangely nothing broke his fall and it felt as through it took an inordinate amount of time to land. He felt himself falling, as if through sky. But land he did, right into semi-darkness, on sharp edged, rocky dirt.

Milo was now squared in a prison cell of soil. Milo was six feet under in a newly dug grave. Suddenly whatever suicidal tendency or what was commonly called a death wish no longer was a part of him. He was now in a frantic panic to hold onto life, dear life, sweet life. He wanted his freedom, his space and every ounce of time he could get. Ray stood at the edge of the freshly dug grave and said, "Hello, dead artist."

But as soon as that was said Paul and Nick took down Ray with the whoosh of a folding chair. And faces appeared all around this frame of dirt, this grave.

Samantha was there, Uncle Allen, Amelia and Becky, and the cousins, and the invited guests.

"Don't worry Milo," Nick said, "I called the police on my cell. We'll get you out of there."

Chapter Thirty-Two

Pablo and Vincent appeared next to him, they both smiled like a host does when they are welcoming a visitor. But Milo was not ready to join the ranks of dead artists.

Milo stood up, and discovered that this grave was deeper than six feet. And then he saw those friends and family members standing on the edge with their hands extended, and all of them wishing he would choose their reaching hands to grasp. But who should he choose? Uncle Allen was over eighty, he certainly didn't have the strength to get Milo out of this mess. Becky and Amelia were reaching and smiling, like two midwives reaching toward a womb, but Milo never knew them to be particularly strong. Emotionally, they were bullish, but physically they were quite weak.

Ray was struggling against those who were trying to restrain him, "Let me the hell go. Get off of me, I'm cool, I just got a little hot under the collar. That's all. Cut me some slack."

Milo was brushing the soil and specs of dirt off his suit while he considered who would have the honor of pulling him out of this open grave.

Then kneeling at the edge he now saw his short, stocky art dealer Nick who was reaching his hand out, like a business executive seeking a firm handshake on a verbal agreement.

"Look, Milo, " said Pablo. "Your dealer is trying to save you."

"Don't worry, you'll get out of this one," Vincent added.

At last they let go of Ray. It occurred to Milo that the one person that got him in this predicament might be the only one strong enough to get him out, Ray seemed to read his mind as he said, "Come on. I put you in there, I can get you out."

Milo looked at his brother's face, tanned by the California sun and etched with disappointment, cheeks creased from the false smile of a disillusioned spirit, eyes widened and hoping for forgiveness.

"No, don't reach for his hand, that would be a terrible mistake," Pablo said.

"You can't trust your brother Milo, haven't you learned that by now?" Vincent added.

And so Milo chose to ignore their warnings and he reached for, not his agent's hand, nor his sister's hand or Donny's or one of the invited guest's, but his brother's, and just as he touched Ray's hand Milo experienced another jolt of "posanoia" (that positive twist on paranoia where one believes that the whole world and everyone in it are not after you and are not against you but are FOR you and that everybody wants only to help).

Ray couldn't lift Milo out alone. It took the grip of a second set of hands to hoist Milo upward from the freshly dug grave. Paul the half-brother, sailor, hang glider, the scuba diver, put both of his hands around Milo's left wrist, while Ray held with both hands Milo's right wrist. It was good brother and bad brother now both working in unison. Yin and Yang.

"Gotcha!" Paul said. And Milo remembered in California when the three of them had sailed together to Catalina Island and the mast broke in half and they were stranded in the Pacific waters. He remembered how Paul had tried to shoot his SOS flare and how the trigger jammed. The three of them sat in the baking August sun, the light blazing. Yes, it was a Sunday, just like today his wedding day and the day of his mother's funeral. He remembered how Paul's boat simply tread water, until help came in the form of a passing barge that towed them in.

Now his two big brothers hoisted him up from the grave.

Chapter Thirty-Three

So this was what became of the marriage and funeral ceremony.

It was a travesty as expected. Ray had once again shown his dark colors and had lost control and ruined everything.

The moment, that hot, yet lovely afternoon prior to Ray's rude interjection of crude talk was perfect in its way, until Ray had shattered it. There was no going back. No pretending it had not happened. And anyway, going backwards was no bargain either.

Once Milo was safely hoisted and standing above ground, the whole group that had followed the ruckus now found themselves precariously huddled around some stranger's grave site. In fact it was the grave site of: *Mr. Lee Ronsen, beloved husband, and father of Dotty, Celia, and Dora. Rest in Peace* with today's date.

Milo read these words on the grave stone and felt an eerie intimacy with this unknown man who once was a husband and a father and who was still beloved, and whose body was probably on its way from the morgue or the funeral parlor.

He thought of his own father...still dead.

Samantha helped Milo dust himself off, but his gray suit was browned and soiled.

"What happened there?" Samantha said to Milo.

"Ray happened." was Milo's answer.

"Does he always do that?"

"Yes he does, I should have warned you."

199

Ray was attempting to withdraw his anger and now make up for what he had done. But he was still acting erratic and high strung and just plain drunk when he made an announcement using his cupped hands as a megaphone. He spoke in abrasive staccato, breaking up the syllables of his speech for emphasis. And this was as equally disheartening to witness as the scuffle that had resulted in Milo's butt first fall into Mr. Ronsen's waiting gravesite.

Ray said, "Please ev-er-y-one, I ap-ol-ogize- with all my heart, please let us go back to what we were do-ing before I..well..I blew ev-ery-thing. Come now, I pro-mise I won't act up a-gain!" Then he went back to a more normal speech pattern when he added, "I guess I just had a long uncomfortable flight here. There was a stop over in Chicago, or Detroit, I can't remember, that was really annoying. I had an Arney's roast beef sandwich that really turned my stomach and gave me gas and bile. I know that's no excuse, but I sat there at the airport for six hours and all I had to entertain myself was a Nicholas Sparks novel...anyhow please everyone, right this way."

The crowd, like meek sheep, slowly waddled back to the folding chairs and the podium, where the interrupted ceremony had taken place. Mrs. Sonas sat alone. Milo was deeply disappointed in Consuelo for leaving his mother alone. He turned to her and said in broken English, "Why you no stay with my Mother?"

Becky who was equally upset translated for him, and Consuelo was visibly ashamed of herself. Her only response was to shrug her shoulders in shame.

Now Milo was losing his temper. "That woman can be so damn stupid."

"Hey watch it," Becky said. "She can understand more English than she lets on."

DEAD ARTIST

"I don't care, she just left our terminally ill mother in the sweltering heat, totally alone."

The guests began to take their seats in the folding chairs, and Milo walked over to his mother to console her, but she didn't seem bothered by what transpired. She looked to be doing what she often did around this time and that was taking a siesta, a cat nap. Milo sat on one side of her and Samantha on her other and Milo said this while pushing back his mother's dry white hair, "It's okay now Mom. Ray said he was sorry and I don't mind, I really don't. This always happens with him...and with me. Now let's try to enjoy the part of the ceremony that you requested. Okay? It's time for your service. Becky and Amelia have something prepared and so does Luna, I do too and I am even sure that Ray has his two cents he wants to add."

Mrs. Sonas seemed to be sleeping, her body bent over like a deflated balloon.

"Look, it's okay now," Amelia said joining them. Becky and Paul also stepped close.

Milo with two fingers lifted her face up by the chin. What they saw on their mother's face was disquieting. For it was then that her children witnessed again that same facial expression their grandmother had at the end. On their mother's face was a frown so exaggerated it looked like a velvet painting of a sad clown. It was that singular expression that comes over a person when they are expecting a loved one or a dear friend at the door during a holiday, and instead at the door stands a ski masked maniac with a pistol aimed directly at their face. Yes, their grandmother had exactly the same fearful and heartbreaking distortion of her features which told of ultimate fear, disappointment and doom all mixed together. Suddenly Sonia Sonas exhaled and her face seemed to lose its elasticity as if she hit the wall of oblivion. Everyone around her began to cry and scream as if they could stop her passing or perhaps they simply wanted to let her know that they were here for her. But it was too late.

"Mother?" Milo said, and then like a crash of a cold wave in the Pacific Ocean, he felt a chill overcome her and she shook, as if from an aftershock. Then she was still. She was gone. It was over. And then just as that truth overtook him, next came the anger at his brother. Ray was to blame! Ray had destroyed everything! Ray! It was always Ray who killed things!

Milo got up and walked over to Ray, who had been oblivious to what just happened, and to his mother's passing and was instead attempting to make small talk with a female guest he had just met for the first time.

This time Milo swung first.

Ray took the blow directly to the face then turned back to face Milo head on, "Why did you do that?"

"You killed her."

Milo swung wildly again, this shot hit Ray squarely in the left eye. Ray lost his balance for a moment, but he neither raised his hand to defend himself nor to retaliate.

"She is gone now," Milo said.

Ray looked past Milo and saw his mother slumped in her seat, surrounded by desperate family and friends. They fumbled with her, not knowing exactly how to tend to somebody that was already gone.

"Oh my God," he said.

"Because of you she spent the last moments of her life watching us fight and everyone left her alone."

"Well, wasn't that nurse supposed to stay with her?"

"It doesn't matter now. She died alone."

"Maybe she wasn't alone at the moment when she died. Maybe she was experiencing a memory, perhaps she was thinking about something nice?"

DEAD ARTIST

Milo couldn't believe that Ray could be that flippant. But still his comment made Milo wonder, "Like just what do you think she was thinking about?" Milo felt tears cloud his eyes.

"Oh it could have been so many things. Maybe she was thinking about that tree over there and how Uncle Allen could take something like that and carve and sand it into something smutty, like a woman's ass." Ray was actually in his demented way, trying to soothe Milo's overflowing emotions, as he tried to control his own.

Milo, Samantha and Luna overhearing this, couldn't help themselves from chuckling. Then Amelia stood between the two feuding brothers and said, "Come on, let's get her out of here. Let's take her home. You know how much she loves....ah loved...her dream house."

Milo:

Mother is gone now, forever.

I am leaving Gold Haven now for good, there is nothing here for me anymore. Samantha understands that what happened between us was, nothing, really. Just a facade of completeness, a parade of an illusion just for mother. The truth is my life is still wonderfully incomplete. I am back in New York again. I guess I have come full circle. This town is jam-packed with people that seem to know me. I am approached often, they ask if I am Milo Sonas, and I say that I am. I am liked. Is this "posanoia" or is it just fame? Sometimes I wonder.

New York City coffee is good, and strong, it feels like it is pushing me, no, not shoving me as my brother did onto the hard soil, but instead I feel I am now falling forward into life and into my true self.

Samantha is a friend now. Don't get me wrong. It's okay this way. She has a lot of time to find someone. She doesn't need me. I have less time.

We laugh a lot when we think about our love making in the past. And when I walk through Union Square it seems everyone is selling stuff, vending anything from artwork to jewelry to handbags. I feel like I was once a pioneer, it used to be just me selling my art at Union Square. Waiting. And now it's here, all that I have waited for. The fame. I enjoy it. The attention... sure. And now I do what I have always done. Charge up on a good cup of coffee, fill a plate with paint, blue, yellow, orange, and on and on. There is always enough paint now. And more than enough space and light to paint in this loft. Pablo just couldn't handle it anymore, watching me paint, while he was unable to do anything but drink espresso and smoke. So Pablo stepped out to buy a pack of cigarettes from the Korean grocer on the corner and never came back. Vincent really hit it off with Samatha's friend Carly. The two of them are always spending time together and neglecting their friends, which is almost as total a disappearance as Pablo's, except some times I see Vincent and his girl walking out on the New York streets, her hand in his back pocket. Lucky Vincent. Maybe when they finish this initial bonding period they will spend more time with me. I don't know. From the look he had on his face, I sense that Pablo might have been mistaken when he told me that dead artists can't feel touch or affection. I believe that Vincent can feel love now. I really do. I hope so anyway.

I was so surprised they hit it off. Carly seemed like such an standoffish girl to me at first. But Samantha explained the reason her friend got along so famously with Vincent was because, well, Carly was involved in a fatal accident years ago. A drunk driver swerved at midnight, on a Thursday night. Carly did not survive long enough even for the paramedics to have a chance to revive her. I guess maybe if you don't find your soul mate in this life there is still hope in the next.

Dead girl loves dead artist.

Dr. Hyatt and I are still in touch, but ever since he lost his license and because there is a now a law that dictates that he cannot practice without one, it makes it impossible for us to meet in person. But we once and for the last time broke that the law and met face to face. I consider him like Vincent and Pablo, to be one of my many fathers.

But he is still alive. Quite old, but still here in this world.

Chapter Thirty-Four

This is what Milo and Dr. Hyatt talked about:

Milo said, "I keep wondering what she was thinking at the end of her life. It's just awful that she had to see her two sons fighting and then she was just left there in the searing heat to die."

"It's okay," Dr. Hyatt said, a simple glass of milk on the iron table in front of him. They were meeting at a place on Avenue A right across the street from Thompson Square Park called Cafe Pick Me Up. He was all bent over from advance scoliosis, but dapper in his second hand suit and tie. "I believe people just want to be alone when they die. I know I would want to be..ah, well... "

"What?"

"Alone."

"When you die?"

"Yes."

"I wonder what I will be thinking about in my last moments."

"It's hard to know. By the way, do you still see Picasso, and Van Gogh around?"

"No not really. Picasso just kind of skipped town, and Van Gogh is in love. I set him up you know."

"It's probably for the best. That phenomena of yours was not really something you could share with many people."

"Samantha could see them."

"Oh yes, Samantha. How is she?"

"She is getting her Masters in photography, or something, I am not sure.... And, she is happy."

"That's nice."

"You know Dr. Hyatt, I have had many fathers in my life. And you too have been like a father to me. I just want you to know that."

"Thank you. I am flattered." He sipped his milk, a bit got on his upper lip. Then he asked Milo, "Tell me, how many mothers have you had?"

"Only one."

"That's nice," Dr. Hyatt said. "With so many fathers, how do you know which was the real one?"

Milo just smiled.

"By the way, I guess that makes you a bastard."

"No, it makes me what my mean ex-girlfriend used to call me... a *bastardo*."

"From now on I will call you Bastardo."

And like two old friends, they shared a laugh in the afternoon.

#DeadArtist

Join in the online discussion of this book by going to www.twitter.com and typing #DeadArtist in the search box at the top. To add to the discussion, simply add #DeadArtist to the end of your tweet.

About the Author

Ivan Jenson's *Absolut Jenson* painting was featured in *Art News*, *Art in America*, and *Interview magazine* and he has sold several works at Christie's, New York. His poems have appeared in *Word Riot*, *Zygote in my Coffee*, *Camroc Press Review*, *Haggard and Halo*, *Poetry Super Highway*, *Mad Swirl*, *Alternative Reel Poets Corner*, *Underground Voices* Magazine, *Blazevox*, and many other magazines, online and in print. Jenson is also a Contributing Editor for *Commonline* magazine.

33666423R00124

Made in the USA
Middletown, DE
22 July 2016